THE ISLAND OF SHADOWS

Dark Relics Series

BOOK 3

RON RIPLEY

EDITED BY ANNE LAO
AND DAWN KLEMISH

ISBN: 979-8-89476-297-5
Copyright © 2025 by ScareStreet.com

Enter the Realm of Terror…

We'd like to take a moment to thank you for your support and invite you to join our VIP newsletter.

Dive deeper into the darkness with exclusive offers, early access to new releases, and bone-chilling deals when you sign up at www.ScareStreet.com.

Let the nightmares begin…

See you in the shadows,
Scare Street

THE WOMAN OF THE SNOW

Yuta Tanaka was pretty sure he was lost.

The lights of the city had fallen behind nearly an hour ago, and the first heavy snow was falling. Night was drawing in, and Tanaka was increasingly uncertain of the route. He had spent most of the afternoon cajoling his local contact to share information on the Sanagi cult. The man, a retired cop, had been evasive. Even the tried and tested combination of cash and booze had taken hours to work its magic. So it was that Tanaka had set out late on a December afternoon, heading inland, toward the mountains.

He could just turn back; the snow was a good excuse. All day, random flakes had drifted down from a sea of low clouds, threatening worse to come. It was snowing in earnest now, with great flurries almost blinding him as they challenged the windshield wipers of Tanaka's rental car. Sure, the Toyota SUV had snow tires—he'd made sure of that—but here in the north of Japan, roads could be blocked by huge snowdrifts after just a few hours. If he kept going, he might become trapped. Every winter, some idiot froze to death in the "snow country", as the locals called it. Tanaka had never thought that idiot might one day be him.

But even as he assessed the situation as a rational adult, his conscience plagued him. The Shadow Trust had given him a mission, and Tanaka was not a man to neglect his duty. It was that sense of fealty to his faraway masters that kept him driving uphill, toward the supposed location of the cult's stronghold. But after another ten minutes or so, reality asserted itself, and Tanaka hit the brakes. The wipers were struggling, and he could barely see to turn the car around. He had to get back to the city, even if it meant reporting abject failure to London.

The shame and loss of face would be terrible. To report failure to the Trust would shame him in the eyes of his senpai. The Englishman was a legendary figure in the world of paranormal research. But the truth was all too apparent. Tanaka had moved too slowly to find Sanagi's elusive followers. The trail had proved too long and tortuous. He was inadequate for the task. The humiliation burned, and he felt his soul shrivel in misery.

"No!" He banged the heel of his hand on the steering wheel. "No. Focus on the here and now."

Tanaka gingerly maneuvered the SUV on the narrow country road, opening the driver's window and sticking his head out into a raging blizzard. Icy flakes stung his cheeks. Some settled on his eyelashes and did not melt, instead forming a white fringe that partly obscured his vision. There was a bump, possibly due to the vehicle hitting a rock. Tanaka thought he had not gone into a ditch, as the car had not tilted. He stopped reversing and changed into low gear. For a gut-wrenching second, he heard wheels spin before the Toyota jerked forward. He turned carefully, easing the car around until he was facing downhill.

His headlights showed nothing but swirling whiteness. He would have to drive at a snail's pace. Tanaka shivered and closed the window again. Then, he eased his foot onto the gas pedal, and the Toyota edged forward. A few seconds later, the rear wheels slewed to the left. The snow had already become treacherous, and his path lay downhill. He stopped, tried again, and panicked slightly as he almost lost control.

The car slid to a halt. Tanaka tried his phone to see if he could get a tow truck or maybe the cops. But, as he'd feared, service was nonexistent. Likewise, his GPS could not tell him where he was. Still, he had the car heater and could get a sleeping bag from the trunk. It wasn't so bad. With almost a full tank of gas, he could keep the battery charged.

He glanced at the dash and felt a chill colder than the blizzard grip him. The gas tank wasn't almost full; it was half-empty. Tanaka stared down at the glowing indicator. Why hadn't he checked before leaving Aomori? How long would the engine run before it conked out? And what then? He had to risk driving despite the skid risk. But if he put the car into a ditch, he'd be certain to freeze.

The snow was easing up a little, providing a small source of hope. His headlights now showed the road a few dozen yards ahead. He put the car back into gear and tried to ease forward, but now, the wheels just spun in snow too deep to negotiate. It seemed impossible, but he was stuck.

Something crossed the road just ahead of him. A pale shape, moving swiftly at the very edge of visibility. Tanaka thought of bears, which were becoming bolder these days, according to the news. He could see the headline now: "Kyoto man apparently eaten by bears". The shape came into view again. It was too slender to be a bear, and it was standing upright, totally still. Then, the blizzard intensified, and the figure was lost to sight.

I must be near a village, or maybe a hotel, Tanaka thought. *There are ski resorts and that kind of thing.*

It would be absurd to freeze to death a short walk from a warm bed, but he had no idea in which direction help might be found. Then he saw the pale figure again, moving off to his left. Tanaka made an impulsive decision. He zipped up his heavy winter coat, put on his gloves, and got out of the car. The cold wasn't quite as bad as he'd feared, but it still numbed his face in seconds. He got a heavy flashlight out of the trunk and went around in front of the vehicle, waving the flashlight beam from side to side.

"Hey!" he shouted. "Hey, wait!"

The figure was just barely visible, no longer stationary but moving slowly away.

"Hey!" Tanaka clumsily made his way through the snow, which was already deep enough to drift. A few straggling trees came into view, and the pale stranger vanished behind one. Something about the figure's movement suggested it was a woman. That, in turn, sounded a warning bell somewhere in the back of his mind. But the night and the blizzard were leaching heat from his feet and hands. He had no time to ponder anything but survival.

Tanaka ran as best he could, kicking up great fans of newly fallen snow, and trying to keep the pale form in sight. His flashlight was powerful but still could not penetrate the swirling blizzard. It had maybe eased up a little, but the snow was now at least a foot deep, and a terrible numbness was creeping up his legs.

A flash of light brought him up short. The light vanished, then reappeared as Tanaka swept the flashlight around. He realized it was a reflection, the beam bouncing back at him from a window. A building was ahead. His spirits rose. As he got closer, his flashlight illuminated more windows, large ones. He barked his shin on a low wall enclosing a snow-shrouded garden. It was either a large private house or a hotel. Either way, he would be sure of help, perhaps even a cup of warm saké and a meal.

But then, doubts arose. The building was dark, but it was still early in the evening. Surely, some lights should be visible. As Tanaka got closer, the truth dawned on him. The building had long since been abandoned. A sign proclaimed the place a hotel, but it was crooked and weather stained.

Tanaka cursed. But any shelter was better than nothing. If he got out of the snow, he might still find a bed. He stumbled toward the big double doors. They were locked, of course, but he was determined to get inside. It was that or hypothermia. He raised his flashlight and struck a glass door panel. It took several blows, but he eventually shattered it, knocking out some wicked-looking shards, and climbing through the gap.

The place was dark and forlorn inside. Cobwebs hung here and there, silvered by frozen moisture. A reception desk and a few pieces of furniture in the atrium confirmed that it had been a hotel. Many had been built during Japan's boom years, only to be abandoned when the property bubble burst. Now that he was out of the driving snow, Tanaka felt the numbness leaving his hands and feet.

Where had the mysterious figure in white gone? He didn't care. Perhaps it was a homeless person who lived around here. He knew such people were generally harmless, and he was in no condition to fight anyone anyway. He picked his way along a corridor, checking empty rooms. Eventually, he found one in which an old mattress had been left leaning against a wall. It was better than nothing. He pulled the shabby mattress over him and lay on the hard floor. He was suddenly very tired and managed to doze off.

Tanaka woke to a strange light streaming in through the dirty window of the room. The sky seemed alive with green and blue fire. The snow had stopped, and the sky was clear, with a handful of bright stars visible through the celestial light show. Tanaka raised himself on his elbows to gaze at the amazing spectacle. A half-forgotten term surfaced in his confused mind.

Aurora Borealis.

He had never seen the Northern Lights. He was far to the north, but this was unprecedented. As he watched, the great curtain of radiance shimmered and flowed. Then it began to assume a very different shape. A dragon-like creature formed, reaching across the sky. Tanaka told himself that he was imagining it, projecting old stories about heavenly beasts onto a random pattern. But the aurora seemed very much like a seven-headed beast, rampant above its earthly domain.

"It is Yelbeghen," said a gentle, melodious voice.

Tanaka twisted around under the mattress and flicked on the flashlight. The doorway framed a woman dressed in white, her face startlingly pale, and her eyes and hair black as night. She was wearing a dress that reached to her feet and seemed grossly inadequate in the piercing cold.

"What… who are you?" he demanded.

The woman did not answer but walked slowly into the room. She smiled down at him as he tried to get to his feet. But tiredness and cold made him clumsy, and he fell, dropping the flashlight. The strange woman knelt by him, holding out a delicate hand.

"Do not be afraid, lost traveler." She looked up at the window where the monstrous dragon thing was fading. "It is an omen of a terror you will not see."

"Who are you?" he asked again. "Are you one of Sanagi's followers?"

The woman tilted her head in a coquettish gesture. She was very beautiful, Tanaka thought. But something about her quelled passion. The coldness in the room seemed to have increased.

"I follow no one." He saw no cloud of breath in front of her mouth as she spoke. Her voice was cold and pure as the ice on a frozen mountain lake.

Suddenly, he knew what she was. A creature of the snow country, a being that sucked the life from unwary men. He had feared bears, ghosts, and lunatics, but this was peril of a far higher order. A snow vampire.

"Yuki Onna!" he exclaimed.

He unfastened his jacket to get at his iron dagger, cursing his lack of foresight. If only the weapon had been lying close at hand. The woman had moved closer, crawling across the dirty floor, her long hair halfway hiding her inhuman beauty. Tanaka's hand touched the grip of the dagger just as her long fingers grasped his wrist. The burning coldness of her touch left his arm useless. He tried to punch her in the face with his left fist, but he might as well have been striking a marble statue for all the effect it had. The Yukki Onna merely smiled, seized his left hand, and—in a single heartbeat—drained all the living warmth from it. He cried out in pain and terror. She pushed him down and straddled him, leaning forward to whisper in his ear.

"Do not be sad, mortal one. For all must perish soon, whether in ice or fire. For this corrupt world is spinning into the wondrous, dreadful age of Yelbeghen. Now join your ancestors, as is right and proper."

And then she wound slender arms around him and kissed him to death.

CHAPTER 1

THE REVENGE OF STINKY JIM

"Gotta love traditional American cuisine."

Craig Ellison looked around the restaurant kitchen, noting smears of grease and burnt patches here and there. As burger joints went, he thought, this one seemed truly forlorn. The lights were not quite bright enough, the fixtures were old, and the décor was tired and faded. If the place was ever featured in a movie, it would have to be a gangster flick set in the seventies. Or maybe a screwball comedy. Not a romance, though. Nobody in their right mind would bring a date here.

"So, he manifests himself in here, Ed?" he asked the manager.

Ed was around forty and looked as if he consumed a lot of his own product. He dabbed at his sweaty forehead with a napkin.

"Yeah, I guess. I mean, he kind of stinks the whole place out, you know? Customers complain. A lot. But it's mostly in the back—the kitchen, the toilets. And outside by the dumpster, of course."

Craig nodded and then closed his eyes and took a deep breath.

"What… what are you doing?" Ed asked.

"Trying to focus," Craig said. "If I could have some quiet?"

"Sure," the manager said. "I'll leave you to it."

Craig heard Ed's heavy footsteps recede, and then the kitchen door closed. He tried to find a trace of the ghost, a hint that this place was haunted. Normally, this was easy. He'd been operating as a freelance exorcist for nearly two months and had earned a few thousand bucks. In general, people wanted ghosts gone, and Craig could oblige in most cases.

This one might be tricky.

"Come on, where are you?" he muttered.

Craig ran through the details of the haunting again. A homeless guy called Jim had stopped by the burger place a few times a week. The staff had taken to giving him food and coffee for free. Then, the old manager had retired and the new boss—the fat guy—had nixed handouts for vagrants. Jim had come in to buy a cheeseburger and coffee to go. He had cash he'd gotten by begging, but the boss man had thrown Jim out, shoving him onto the sidewalk.

"The guy hadn't washed for, like, months, maybe years." Ed was irate at the memory of the incident. "He stank like old garbage! I couldn't let someone like that inconvenience my customers, now, could I?"

Craig had resisted the urge to point out that Jim had been a customer.

Ed had thrown Jim out one night in late December, not long before Christmas. An unusually heavy snowfall had struck the town that night. Early the following morning, Jim's body had been found in the alley out back. "Curled up like a baby," according to the jogger who'd spotted the corpse. A few days later, a bad smell had turned up. It had grown steadily worse and gotten the burger joint a series of bad reviews. Now, the place was almost dead most nights.

A local journalist had covered the story in a half-jokey way. The piece was headlined "Is this the Revenge of Stinky Jim?". Meanwhile, the boss man had called in a minister, a priest, and then a rabbi, but it seemed that Jim was impervious to religious exhortations. Craig was, it seemed, the last resort. A guy who conducted ghost tours and claimed to be able to speak to the dead. Ed had made it clear that he felt Craig was probably a charlatan or mentally ill, but he was at the end of his tether.

"Hey, if you can persuade him to get lost, you can eat here free for a month."

That had been the original offer. Craig had declined it in favor of cash. After some haggling, a price had been agreed upon. Now, all that remained was to persuade a soul who'd been hassled by the cops innumerable times to move on one last time. To go to a better place.

The problem was, to achieve that, Craig needed a ghost's cooperation. And, at the moment, there was no sign of Jim turning up to give it.

"Come on, Jim," he sighed, opening his eyes. "You must know that I'm here. I know that you know I'm here. You're keeping an eye on the place, right? So you can cause maximum trouble for Ed."

A slight breeze ruffled a discarded wrapper on the untidy counter by the serving hatch. Then, a pungent smell assailed Craig's nostrils. It combined sweat, urine, and less pleasant odors. Stinky Jim was nearby. The smell became a stench so intense that it seemed to make the air around Craig denser. The ghost seer had never been in a sewer on a hot summer's day, but he imagined it might be like this.

"Jeez, Jim," he said. "Dial it back a little."

He tried pinching his nose. As he'd expected, it made no difference. The odor was psychic in nature, affecting the olfactory part of the brain. Craig had long ago given up on grasping the science of it all, but it was clear that nothing could block out Stinky Jim. Craig was glad he'd not eaten anything since lunchtime, as he might have brought up his meal at this point.

"Aw come on, buddy," he wheedled. "This is no way to spend a perfectly good afterlife. Sure, the fat guy was a jerk, and he should be punished. But what about the staff? The people who were kind to you? What about the ordinary folks who just want a burger? Have some sense of proportion. Leave the guy's punishment up to some higher authority, you know? Because one day, he'll take the same path you did."

The stench receded a little, and Craig felt he could breathe almost normally. The lights flickered, went out, and came back on at reduced wattage. Energy was being drained somehow. The temperature in the narrow, low-ceilinged kitchen fell by a couple of degrees in seconds. Then, the shadow cast by the huge refrigerator by the grill seemed to grow deeper and started to flow out toward Craig. Gradually, the darkness took form.

Colors, albeit dull and washed out, started to show. A pale oval blur became a face. A smiling face.

Stinky Jim looked benignly at Craig. That was a plus.

"Hi," the ghost said. "What's that mean bastard paying you for this?"

Craig named the sum, and added, "I get nothing up front; it's only by results. So, maybe you could help me out here? The living have bills to pay."

Jim crossed his arms and studied Craig, who reciprocated. The ghost looked almost entirely like a living man. Jim had been small in life, maybe five-six and skinny, but with a wiry look about him. In the gloom, it was hard to tell, but Craig thought Jim had pale blue eyes. There was a humorous upturn to his mouth and laugh lines on his thin face. Not a bad guy, at a guess. One of those you met for a beer and could shoot the breeze with. A good pal who liked a joke. Hardly your standard vengeful phantom. The only clue that Jim was not alive was the way he faded out a little below the knees.

"You'll have to do better than that," Jim said. "I want that dirtbag to lose his job. And if this place closes, so what? It's a prime site. They'll just reopen it as a Burger King or whatever."

"Or maybe they'll think the site is haunted and not bother. The place might be empty for years in the present economic climate," Craig found himself saying.

"Wow, you sound like a newsreader," Jim said, wide-eyed.

They laughed together, which was encouraging.

"Okay." Craig held up his hands in mock surrender. "If you want to put him out of business, I can't stop you. But have you considered that revenge is kind of mean-spirited? No pun intended."

Jim pondered that and then shook his head. Craig could feel several hundred dollars slipping from his grasp.

"Is there nothing I can say to change your mind?"

"No, but there's something *he* can say," Jim said, and explained what he meant.

A minute later, Craig went out into the restaurant and spoke to the manager. At first, Ed was stubborn, resentful, and refused to cooperate. But Craig wore him down after a while.

"It's the only way to save the business," he repeated. "And it's not much to ask."

He led the manager back into the kitchen, where Jim was waiting by the fridge. The manager seemed to sense the ghost's location, staring uncertainly in Jim's direction.

"Go on," Craig said. "He's waiting."

The fat man cleared his throat self-consciously.

"I'm sorry," he said in a monotone. "I'm sorry I threw you out. Jim."

Craig groaned inwardly as Jim shook his head.

"Not good enough," the ghost said. "No way does that cut it! It was totally insincere. What a jerk!"

Craig repeated the words to the manager, who bridled at the rebuke.

"Goddamn it, all I said was that the guy stank! And he did! He friggin' stank to high heaven!"

The pungent odor grew more intense, almost suffocating. The manager's eyes watered, and he started to gasp. Jim moved toward the fat man, reaching out with pale, dirty hands.

"No!" Craig cried, interposing himself between the two. "You're better than that, Jim!"

He felt an icy sting as ghostly fingertips brushed against him. Ghosts could not kill him, but they could still inflict pain. But in this case, he felt he had correctly gauged the phantom's character. He turned his back on Jim, confident that the ghost wished him no harm, and confronted the manager.

"The last words he heard in his entire life were yours." Craig felt a surge of anger that surprised him. "The last thing a human being said to him before he died! Can you imagine that? How would you like that, Ed?

12

Huh? If you were down on your luck, sick in your mind or body or both, lost and unloved in a cold, harsh world, and then the one person who could have helped you through a cold winter's night degraded you instead? Compared you to trash? To garbage? To filth?"

Craig was shouting now.

"Let me go!" the manager squeaked.

Craig realized that he had grabbed the front of the man's shirt and pushed him up against the counter. He let go and stammered out an apology.

"But for God's sake, and yours, do the right thing!" he added.

The manager, still breathless from Jim's horrendous stink, slumped to the floor. For the first time, Craig wondered about the fat man's health. The guy's head lolled to one side, and drool glistened at the corner of his mouth.

"Oh, crap!"

Craig took out his phone and called 911. Halfway through explaining the situation, he was distracted by the sudden appearance of a second ghost in the kitchen. The newcomer was considerably larger than Jim and seemed very confused. As a ghost, Ed looked healthier than he had while alive.

"Okay," Craig said after ending the call. "How are we going to do this? Jim, you wanna go first?"

CHAPTER 2

EXIT ELMER BANTRY

"And then what happened?" Tara asked.

They were sitting outside a small coffee shop next to the park, not far from Craig's apartment.

"I moved them both on, of course," Craig said.

"Yeah, but to where?" Tara persisted, leaning forward. "I'm assuming Jim went somewhere pretty good?"

Craig nodded. He recalled the swirling vortex of light that had appeared above the vagrant's head as he'd begun the process. He'd moved on dozens of spirits since acquiring the power at Grendon Mill. Only a handful had gone to a genuinely bad place. Jim had drifted up to what looked like a farm, or maybe a large suburban house.

"There was plenty of green, anyhow," he told Tara. "Clear blue sky, a dog on the porch that seemed very pleased to see him. I caught a glimpse of a woman coming out of the front door. She was wearing an old-fashioned dress like in a movie from the Fifties. Or one of those magazines about genteel homemaking."

Tara was listening open-mouthed.

"So... maybe that was his childhood? His paradise consisted of all the best memories from the days when everything was fun, and people cared for him?"

"When he had hope and a place in this world." Craig looked down at his half-eaten donut. "When he was loved and knew it."

Tara took a sip of her latte, grimaced, and set it down.

"Yeah, about that last part... I keep getting mixed signals from you,

Craig. You said you wanted to spend time together when we're not working. But you don't want me to stay at your place."

Craig sighed and tried to explain again.

"Billy and Chloe are good friends, but I can't quite trust them not to—well, barge in at awkward moments. Billy, in particular, has his own definition of personal space."

Tara smiled slightly.

"He's the dead biker, right? The one with the occult tattoo?"

Craig nodded.

"The seven-headed dragon. But the point is, I would like us to take things to the next level, it's just awkward."

Tara pushed her coffee away and stared levelly at him.

"I want to take it to the next level, too," she said. "So, since we've got a whole day before Stark turns up, maybe we could go back to my hotel room and have what I believe all the naughty people call a nooner?"

Craig's heart started beating faster than it had in the restaurant kitchen. He felt himself reddening.

"Wow… um, yeah, okay, that would be…"

Somebody was approaching from behind Tara, an oldish man in dark clothes with a clerical collar. Tara twisted around in her seat.

"Is somebody there?" she asked, not seeing the newcomer.

At the same moment, Craig recognized the minister.

"It's okay, it's just old Elmer. The Reverend Elmer Bantry, that is," he explained. "He's kind of an intense, Bible-thumper type. But he's harmless enough."

The dead preacher stopped a few paces from their table, glowering at Craig, and then the phantom jabbed a finger at him and spoke.

"Repent, sinner! Cast aside foul lust and worldly ambition, you limb of Satan, and repent!"

Craig sighed. Why did the religious ones turn up at the worst times?

"Craig?" Tara's voice was barely audible as the preacher ranted about hellfire and punishment.

"I got a live one here—metaphorically speaking," he told her. "Something seems to have gotten him worked up."

Tara stared in Elmer's direction. The preacher looked down at her and pointed a quivering finger.

"The Scarlet Woman!" he boomed. "Whore of Babylon! A witch possessed of unholy powers!"

Craig got up and casually walked around the small table.

"Now, come on, Reverend. That's just downright rude. Let's keep it civilized."

"What's he up to?" Tara looked past the ghost's right ear.

"He's denouncing us," Craig said tactfully. "The usual stuff. Never seen him this agitated, though."

A small cast iron brooch detached itself from Tara's jacket and floated up into the air. The preacher, seeing this, raised his voice still higher. A torrent of Biblical condemnation flooded from his lips, along with flecks of immaterial spittle that vanished in midair.

"Should I give him the treatment?" Tara asked.

"There are people who might see," Craig said quickly. "And he's not a bad guy, he's just a tad excitable."

Tara shrugged, and the brooch floated down onto her outstretched palm.

"Thou shalt not suffer a witch to live!" the ghost howled and lunged at Tara.

Craig was already blocking the move, but unlike Stinky Jim, this ghost had no compunction about harming him. The phantom's body passed into his, and a fierce, painful coldness gripped his innards. Worse still, Elmer's head plunged into Craig's cranium. He got a flash of the ghost's fire-and-brimstone imagination as well as the agony of interpenetration. With a huge effort of will, he thrust the preacher away with his mind and then staggered back and collided with the table.

"You okay?"

Tara got up and clutched his arm.

"Fornication!" the ghost harangued. "Filthy adulterers seeking to slake their lusts. Public displays of wantonness!"

"Aw, shut up!" Craig snapped, then apologized to Tara. "Not you, him. I'm going to see if I can get rid of him."

The dead minister, despite his ongoing monologue, seemed to sense trouble. Bantry produced a small, black book and held it up. It was a Bible, but something about it made Craig do a double-take. The book had a cross embossed on the cover in gold leaf, but the book seemed flimsy, with loose pages falling away as the ghost shoved it in Craig's face.

"Your faith doesn't look too secure, preacher man," Craig said. "Maybe you're having doubts? Can't hang on to your convictions?"

He reached out and grabbed the book, which fell apart. The covers and spine disintegrated into lumps of black soot, setting flimsy leaves spiraling toward the ground. Like the preacher's spittle, the fragments faded to nothing. Bantry stared at Craig, then knelt and clasped his hands together in prayer.

"Oh Lord, protect me from these servants of the Evil One!"

"Stop being dumb and listen to reason for once," Craig said. "Look, I'll help you get to the afterlife you deserve if you just give me five minutes."

He took a breath and then focused his power on a spot above the preacher's head. A small orb of light formed. Tara, sensing what was happening, relaxed her hold on Craig's arm. The dead minister stopped praying and opened his eyes in time to see the colorless orb become a blue-white vortex of light.

Craig had not quite recovered from his encounter at the burger joint the previous day, but he dug deep and found the energy. The glowing whirlpool widened and grew brighter, intense even in the midday sunlight. The ghost was resisting, whining now as much as ranting, but Craig was determined to rid himself of Bantry. The crazed minister was too far gone to be trusted. Innocent people could be killed by such a ghost. Why the preacher had gone barmy was a side issue.

The whirlpool of light widened still more, and the blue-white light became tinged with flecks of orange and red. Now, Craig could see something beyond the portal. It was a church, and a man in clerical garb was preaching to a congregation. The perspective was that of a child looking up from the front row. The scene was almost colorless, lit by a harsh light that emphasized the severe lines of the towering minister's face.

"Daddy!" Bantry whimpered, confirming Craig's first thought. "Daddy, I tried! I tried, but they tempted me. I was weak, and I succumbed…"

The ghost fell to his knees as the portal grew wider, wildly calling upon God to save him. But then, the view above them changed. The scene in the church was replaced by an almost cartoon-like image of heaven, complete with fluffy clouds and pearly gates. A kind-looking man held a book to one side.

Bantry fell silent and then stood and reached skyward with his long, skinny arms. He looked at Craig again. All traces of the ghost's earlier frenzy were gone as he whispered something urgently. Then, a blaze of glorious light spilled out of the portal, dazzling Craig and forcing him to turn away and close his eyes.

"Is he okay?"

A waitress had emerged from the coffee shop while Tara did her best to stop Craig from toppling over. A couple of people strolling nearby had stopped to stare.

"He's fine," Tara insisted. "He just has these little—seizures, kind of. Maybe get him a glass of water?"

The waitress, looking relieved, scuttled back inside. Tara helped Craig to his seat.

"I take it you got rid of the holy roller?"

"Yeah. It was tough at first, but..."

Craig paused while the waitress brought out a glass of water. He was out of it, viewing everything through the wrong end of a telescope. Terrible fatigue afflicted his limbs, so he could barely move. Tara held the glass to his lips and ordered him to drink, so he did.

"We need to get you indoors, so you can lie down." She frowned with worry.

"Old Elmer said something right at the end," Craig said, struggling to form words.

"That can wait." Tara took out her phone. "I'll call an Uber. Hang in there."

But Craig didn't want to wait, as he feared the last thing the ghost had said might fade from his mind. So, he croaked out the warning as best he could.

"The seven-headed beast will consume you."

CHAPTER 3
A WALK IN THE PARK

Craig woke with a throbbing headache to see Tara standing with her back to him. She was whistling what might have been a merry little tune if she hadn't been a quarter-tone flat. He was lying on a double bed in what he concluded was her hotel room. He had a vague recollection of a taxi, an elevator, and being pushed onto the bed. Everything else was a blur.

Craig tried to sit up and failed. His body was still weighed down by tiredness. So many ghosts had approached him for help in recent months. His reserves of power had gradually been drained, and now, his battery was flat.

"Oh, God," he said. "I feel awful."

"Just what a girl likes to hear from a guy in her bed!" Tara said chirpily. She turned around and held up two white mugs.

"Tea or coffee? They put kettles in hotel rooms now; isn't that great? It's because Chinese tourists want tea-making facilities just like the Brits!"

"Coffee," Craig said. "Coffee will be fine. Plenty of sugar. How did you get me here?"

"I'm stronger than I look," she said. "Plus, psychokinesis to stop you from falling over a couple of times. Oh, and that nice waitress helped me get you to the Uber. And a couple of Dutch tourists outside the hotel were very nice: They got you out of the car. They asked if you'd been on the booze, so I just agreed. You were going on about dragons and then you switched to a denunciation of French cheese, for some reason."

Craig pondered that for a moment.

"Oh, that. I had some bad Brie a few years back. I thought I was lactose intolerant for a while. When I Googled it, I found you can't just catch it when you're an adult."

Tara's face showed she was suppressing laughter. She walked to the bed, leaned over, and kissed him on the forehead.

"Don't ever change, esteemed colleague."

They fell silent, looking at each other. Craig felt sure this was the moment when he should say something meaningful, but memories of the Brie incident kept intruding on his confused thoughts. The kettle boiled and switched itself off with a click. Tara made instant coffee for Craig and tea for herself. Then, she moved a chair over so she could sit by the bed.

"So much for the nooner," she remarked wryly. "Still, if you're feeling okay by tomorrow… but of course, we have the meeting."

Craig set the coffee mug by the bedside. He'd forgotten the meeting. They had to check in with Stark at Hannigan's, and, presumably, be given another mission. The money from the last job had been generous, meeting all Craig's rent and other living expenses for nearly six months. If the next job was as lucrative, he might consider not working for Stark anymore.

"Yeah," Tara said, when Craig explained this, "but I don't think he'd be too pleased with that attitude."

Craig had had much the same thought. Peregrine Stark was not a man to cross. There were stories. But, by the same token, assisting the man to amass a collection of occult items felt increasingly like collaborating in a crime. Maybe an atrocity. Stark had the amulet from Grendon Mill and the Celtic sword from Scotland. He was supposedly acting as a middleman to rich collectors, but that story had an odor to it.

"Seven heads of Yelbeghen, seven on that amulet we retrieved." Craig picked up his coffee again. "You think maybe there are seven objects?"

This was covering old ground, but Craig felt the need to discuss it again. He had the possibly irrational conviction that if they kept plugging away at the known facts, they'd achieve some kind of insight.

"Maybe," Tara said. "But he might have most of them already."

Craig murmured his agreement.

"So, if we collect another one, we could be handing him the last piece, or component, or whatever. You think he's bringing this demon or god or whatever into the world?"

Before she could answer, Tara's phone played a snatch of a familiar tune. It signaled a message from a particular individual. She checked and looked up at Craig.

"He's ready for us," she said. "Should I tell him to come up here?"

"No," Craig said. "We might be under surveillance. We don't want Stark to know about…"

He glanced around, wondering if the room was bugged. He was probably just being paranoid, but they had agreed to certain precautions. Like no naming names.

"About our friend."

Tara sat on the bed and felt Craig's forehead, then took his pulse.

"Well, there's nothing obviously wrong with you apart from fatigue, so I'll tell our friend we'll see him in a couple of hours, maybe?"

Two hours later, they returned to the park, but this time, they bypassed the coffee shop and headed for the small lake. Ducks and geese paddled back and forth, and a couple of squirrels shadowed the pair as they passed some dense bushes. Gravel crunched underfoot as they made their way along the water's edge. They had seen no ghosts so far, or at least no obvious ones, though a family paddling a small pedalo on the lake gave Craig pause for thought.

"He didn't specify a place?" Craig asked.

Tara didn't reply but pointed at a bandstand that looked sadly in need of renovation, with signs of weather damage and plenty of graffiti. As they got closer, Craig saw there were holes in the wooden canopy. Around the octagonal base of the bandstand, weeds made their presence felt.

"I guess we wait here." Tara climbed three low steps and walked under the canopy.

Craig followed her and then looked around. A man in a hoodie was standing at the foot of the steps. He had approached in silence despite the gravel pathway.

"Hey." Shane Ryan looked up at Craig. "You look terrible, man. What have you been doing?"

They spent a couple of minutes discussing Elmer Bantry's warning, or prophecy. Shane was interested.

"Ghosts can say all kinds of crazy things to throw you off-balance," he mused. "But if this one was moving on, maybe he had a special insight. Seven heads; that's pretty on point."

They talked some more, and Tara asked if Shane's sources had turned up anything interesting.

"Kind of," he grunted. "One theme I keep getting is that something big is going down in the East."

Tara mulled this over.

"East of where? It's a relative term on a globe."

"Yes, but Yelbeghen is supposed to have risen somewhere in Siberia," Craig pointed out. "That's the Far East, right? Or close, anyhow."

"Yeah," Shane agreed. "I'd say East Asia or Russia is the focus of a lot of attention."

He switched his gaze to Tara.

"How about your contacts in England?"

Tara shook her head.

"No more news of Mortlake. I thought Ellen Grant might help, but she's gone dark. I checked, and she doesn't work at Castle McIvor anymore. I'm guessing she was put there because the Shadow Trust knew someone would come for the sword. The omens or whatever pointed that way. Maybe they intervened on our behalf when we were on their patch, but now, they're watching from a safe distance?"

Craig felt a twinge of annoyance at the mention of the Trust. The London-based organization was supposedly the best in the business of paranormal research, but its loyalties were debatable. Ellen Grant was a Trust operative who had helped them obtain the sword of Laird McIvor. But Marcus Mortlake, Tara's mentor and now also a Trust operative, had steered clear of them when they were in the UK.

"He might not have a choice," Tara said defensively. "He'll always do what's right if he can, but in the end, there's only so much one man can do."

They discussed plans for the next mission. The one point they agreed upon was that Stark should not get the artifact, whatever it was. If possible, they would ask Mortlake to take it into the Trust's protection. If not, they would do their best to either hide it or destroy it if possible. They might, of course, fail to obtain it at all, as Craig pointed out.

"We'll get it," Shane said with steely determination. "I've seen enough and heard enough. And I don't like the idea of raising some Siberian demon. I say we put Stark out of business."

CHAPTER 4
EVERYDAY LIFE AMONG THE DEAD

Craig woke up just after nine the next morning. He was in his own bed and regretted it as never before. He'd done the sensible thing. An exhausted man should get an early night. He hoped Tara would remain keen to take their relationship to the next level.

"You're overthinking it, buddy," Billy said. "You're always overthinking the problem. Be like a bird in flight. Feel the air currents. Gravity. Soar."

Craig had confided in the ghost biker at breakfast. Something about Billy inspired confidence despite the guy's formidable appearance. And the fact he had had been dead for far longer than Craig had been alive. That said, Billy's advice could be terse to the point of rudeness. Billy called this "Zen with attitude".

"So, what do you think I should say to her?" Craig persisted. "I mean, what did you say when you... you know."

Billy, who was peering enviously into Craig's cereal bowl, responded at once.

"I said, 'Hey, sugar, how about it?' But those were different times, my friend."

Chloe, the emo ghost, appeared through the living room wall.

"You should always be open about your feelings," she said earnestly. "And Cheerios are not a proper breakfast for a man of action. You should at least have some toast."

Billy and Chloe began to bicker about suitable breakfasts. Craig, having finished his Cheerios, got up to cook the last of the bacon.

Checking the date on the pack, he saw it had expired yesterday.

"I'll risk it," he said to himself.

"You know the best way to cook bacon." Billy loomed behind Craig as he turned on the stove.

Craig did. One downside of living with the spirits of the dead was that they tended to repeat themselves. Their opportunities for learning new stuff were drastically limited. Sure, they could watch TV or surf the net, but they couldn't eat or drink or travel. It made some ghosts go a little stir-crazy.

"Stark-naked, like a newborn baby," Billy went on. "That way, you never turn the heat high enough to burn it, and it's cooked through properly."

Craig stole a sidelong glance at Chloe. She obliged by producing one of her exaggerated, teenage eyerolls. Chloe was also predictable, but at least she knew it.

"I don't think I could ever do that, Billy," he said. "I'll risk some hot fat spitting at me rather than stand naked in front of…"

He almost bit his tongue. He had been about to say "strangers", and that was an unpalatable half-truth. The living and the dead could interact in many ways, but there were limits. A ghost loving a human, or vice-versa, never ended well. Or at least, Craig had never come across an instance of things working out. He looked at Chloe again and saw her crestfallen expression, made more melancholy by heavy makeup that was permanently streaked with tears. She retreated into the wall.

"Now you've upset her," Billy said needlessly. "Girl like that, she might fall hard for the bad boys, but she'll fall even harder for a nice guy when she finds The One. Hell, I remember this chick down in St. Petersburg…"

Craig tuned out Billy's anecdote and finished cooking the bacon, then made himself a basic sandwich garnished with some distinctly gunky ketchup. Many years of living frugally had left their mark on his eating habits. Maybe a better diet would make it easier for him to move ghosts on without collapsing.

This train of thought was derailed by his phone. It was Tara. She had been contacted by Stark, confirming that the meeting was set for eleven. That was in an hour. Craig had slept long and soundly, and he felt re-energized. He hoped he wouldn't have to move on anyone else between his apartment and Hannigan's. He mentioned this to Billy as he was getting dressed.

"I have a feeling our girl might be asking you for the big boost," the biker said.

Craig stopped searching for a matching pair of socks and stared at the ghost. The thought of losing Chloe gave him a sinking feeling in the pit of his stomach. When he'd first formed his ghost support group, Chloe had been shy and had hardly said a word. But she had gradually come out of her shell, and they'd become friends. She had also helped him with some useful information before his first job for Stark.

"You think she's ready to… to move on?" he asked.

Billy shrugged his broad shoulders.

"Way she's been lately, mooning around, looking even sadder than usual. She said something about meeting old friends, and I guess that means ones who've passed. Seems like quite a few of her pals had tragic lives."

Craig sat on the bed, sock in hand, and wondered if he could bear to move Chloe on. His newfound power had already sent Leroy, by far the friendliest of the old group, to a better place. That was good, of course, but it had deprived Craig of a kindly and sage adviser and confidante. To lose Chloe would leave him bereft of her kindness and gentle humor. Selfishly, he hoped Billy was wrong.

"Hey, we all gotta go sometime," the biker said. "And the things I've been hearing lately, maybe it'd be a good time for me to move on as well."

Craig resumed his sock quest.

"What have you heard? Apart from general prophecies of doom, because we both know those are always going around."

"Yeah." Billy walked over to the bedroom window. "But word on the street is, shit's gonna get real, and real soon."

The way Billy had almost echoed Shane's words brought Craig up short. Rumors spread among the dead as fast and as often as they did among the living. He'd learned this over the years. He'd also learned that the dead, like the living, were far from reliable when it came to passing on juicy titbits of information.

Ghosts might not have social media, but they made up for it with the ability to spy on pretty much everybody. If a ghost in, say, Morocco, saw a magician controlling a ghoul, they would mention it to a pal or two, and those pals would pass it on. Pretty soon, there'd be a wave of ghostly gossip spreading around the globe, and the tale would naturally be corrupted in the telling. The Moroccan mage would become an Algerian adept or maybe an enlightened Egyptian. Instead of a ghoul, the entity concerned might be described as a terrifying vampire or an immensely powerful djinn. The original facts were lost amid exaggeration, error, and downright fabrication.

Craig pointed all this out to Billy.

"I wish your jungle telegraph would give out the plain facts for once," he added.

Billy, still gazing out onto the street below, didn't seem to hear at first. Then, he turned slowly. For the first time, Craig saw immense sadness in the spirit's expression.

"We all believed that hippie shit, you know?" Billy said quietly. "Flower children, love and peace. And look where it got us. The world's on the brink, my friend. On the brink."

Before Craig could think of anything to say, the building opposite became visible through Billy as the ghost's imposing bulk faded. In a couple of heartbeats, the big man was gone, leaving Craig half-dressed and wondering what the future would bring.

Assuming there was one.

CHAPTER 5

WHERE EVERYBODY KNOWS YOUR NAME

The walk to Hannigan's took him through a ghost-heavy area. He encountered a few familiar faces, all belonging to the dead. It might have been chance, but Craig got the impression that the ghosts were avoiding him. Billy's last words haunted him. Was the world on the brink? And if so, on the brink of what?

Craig tried to set thoughts of impending Armageddon aside. First, thinking about it wouldn't help prevent it. Second, he might demoralize himself by contemplating possible disasters. And third, he needed to focus on Stark. Did Stark know about Shane? And if he asked point-blank, would Craig dare deny it? The cunning, self-styled middleman would see through any lies and had many sources of information.

Hannigan's was now two blocks away, and already, Craig saw the signs. The pub was the only place in town—perhaps the only place in the state—which ghosts could not enter. Nor could demons or other paranormal entities. Customers at the old Irish establishment were therefore immune from supernatural persecution or surveillance. But they also had to pass through a kind of gauntlet outside, because a certain type of person hates being told they can't go somewhere.

And that, Craig thought, *goes double for ghosts.*

But it wasn't the ghosts he saw first. No, something else was in the vicinity of Hannigan's, something that seldom allowed itself to be seen. Whatever it was, it seemed harmless to the living, but it regarded the dead as tasty morsels. Today, with the sun high in a cloudless sky, Craig had assumed the lurking entity would not be around. But now he saw a small, dark cloud that hovered over the corner where Hannigan's stood.

This was unusual. Not unheard of, but still a rare event. None of the living seemed to have spotted the weather anomaly, but as he neared the pub, Craig noticed ghosts peering upward in trepidation. They sensed something strange and dangerous was nearby. The cloud, gray and vaguely oval, looked like it had been painted onto an azure ceiling.

Hannigan's came into view. The coterie of spirits around the pub's door and windows was thinner than usual. As he crossed the road, Craig saw that some of them seemed confused, agitated, perhaps even deranged. That would explain why they had entered a danger zone despite the hovering cloud.

Don't let it happen. Not while I'm looking, he thought.

As if on cue, it happened. A long, grayish filament darted down from above and wrapped around one of the ghosts. The spirit, judging by her clothing, had died in the early twentieth century. The ghost waved her arms frantically and screamed for help. She looked straight at Craig. He could do nothing, of course. Nobody could. Nobody dared to deal with any of the lurking things that preyed on ghosts.

The weird tendril hauled the ghost upward at tremendous speed, and the screams were abruptly cut off. Craig wanted to believe that this meant the nameless woman's soul had moved on, but he could never quite convince himself of that. He had heard of beings that consumed and destroyed souls, much like most people devoured animals. But nobody seemed sure what these predators were.

Most of the ghosts gathered around the doorway vanished. Only a couple of the more hopeless phantoms remained. They pawed pitifully at Craig as he dodged past them, trying in vain to avoid their quick, cold touch. He sensed no malice in them, only a desperate desire for admittance. What did they think they would find in Hannigan's? A term Tara had used once sprang to mind. Heartsease. Even ghosts could get tired of existence.

Thoughts of Tara made him stop and look around after he entered the pub. She was nowhere to be seen. Nor was Peregrine Stark. Or so Craig thought at first. Stark had, for years now, treated the end of the bar left of the door as his place of business. At the moment, the stool the shabby dealer occupied so much of the time was vacant. Craig went to the bar and ordered a lite beer.

"You meeting Stark?" Melody, the barmaid, asked.

"Yeah, but he seems to be cutting it close," Craig replied.

The barmaid jerked her head to one side, indicating the booths to the right of the entrance.

"What?" Craig asked, puzzled.

He could not see Stark or Tara. Hannigan's had a traditional vibe and was not brightly lit. Where morning sunlight did not fall, there were deep shadows. But then a stranger sitting in one of the booths to the right waved a hand. Craig squinted at the man.

"Holy crap!" he said.

"*Unholy* crap." The barmaid set Craig's beer in front of him.

He mumbled a thank you and continued to stare. The beckoning stranger was Peregrine Stark. But this was Stark transformed. He was no longer dressed like he'd just come from a thrift store. Instead of an array of mismatched, secondhand garments, Stark now wore a matching dark blue jacket and pants. As Craig walked toward Stark, he saw the other man also had on a shirt and tie. The whole ensemble was understated but spoke of money and care. Did Stark have a personal shopper now?

"Ah, Craig, always on time or even a little early! Such punctuality is laudable in these louche times!"

Smiling broadly to expose what looked like capped teeth, Stark stood and proffered a hand. Craig took it automatically, noting that the man's flesh was dry and supple, and his grip was strong. But it was Stark's face that confused him. Clean-shaven, with well-defined cheekbones and a strong jawline, it suggested the man had had work done. A lot of work. Stark could afford it.

"Please, take a seat. Ms. Pride paid a visit to the little girl's room. When she emerges, we can begin."

Craig set down his beer and sat, trying not to stare but failing.

"I trust I find you well?" Stark asked.

"Oh, yeah, I'm fine," Craig replied. "You're looking good. Been working out?"

The question seemed downright absurd, if not insulting, but Stark took it in good part and chuckled.

"I've been working out a lot of things, you could say. Thanks to you, in large part, I have entered a new phase of my… career."

Craig noted that the man's voice also seemed stronger than before, not to mention a little deeper. Magic sprang to mind. Some kind of Faustian bargain, perhaps, that had rejuvenated and invigorated the once-shabby Stark.

"Ah, here she is!" Stark looked toward the bar.

Tara was approaching. Like Craig, she had favored casual attire, and so they both seemed underdressed next to the new-look Stark. As she scooched in beside Craig, Tara managed a smile for their employer.

"Guess we're all here," she said. "So, it's down to business."

"Quite so!"

Stark took out a piece of paper and unfolded it.

"Your next objective. I will, of course, send you a jpeg, but I think a hard copy carries more weight, somehow."

Tara reached over and pulled the sheet toward them. Craig was disappointed with the picture. It was a monochrome drawing, evidently taken from a book. The object depicted was unremarkable, just a dark lump of rock that might have been a badly damaged sculpture. The shape hinted at a form that had been mutilated. Several circular patches were on top of the vaguely rectangular object where damage had occurred. There was a caption underneath the drawing in what might have been Chinese characters. Craig recalled the rumor of something arising in the East.

"You could find something like that in the nearest quarry," Craig said half to himself. "Or a junk shop, maybe, depending on the size."

Stark wagged a well-manicured finger in mock reproof.

"Now, now; don't judge a book by its cover. It is a thing of great power and spiritual importance. A true mystical artifact, its origins lost in the mists of time."

"What is it?" Tara asked bluntly.

Stark's affable expression turned serious.

"It is sometimes called the Sanagi Relic, after a certain Japanese gentleman. But its more correct appellation is the Idol of Yelbeghen."

CHAPTER 6
SEEK THE SEVEN-HEADED GOD

"The Sanagi cult," Stark explained, "emerged in the late nineteenth century after Japan was forced to open to the West. Most people accepted that, but others reacted—badly. Very badly."

"I've seen that movie," Craig said. "So, this Sanagi guy was, what? A samurai who didn't want the old ways to end?"

Stark shook his head.

"No, he was a monk of the Shinto religion. Shinto venerates many gods, all of them benign to some degree. But Sanagi felt his faith was too weak to oppose Westernization. He believed his culture was under threat and formed a deep, abiding hatred of all things foreign. Especially all things American. And European, for good measure."

"So, he was a fanatical nationalist?" Tara asked. "That never ends well."

This time, Stark made a noncommittal noise.

"Hmm, I suppose you could call him that, but he was very unorthodox. He believed Japan could never beat the West at its own game—militarism, colonial empires, and so forth. Instead, Sanagi felt that supernatural powers should be invoked to purge the country of all foreign influences. But the irony is that the power he sought was not in Japan. It was to be found in—"

"Siberia," Craig interrupted. "Yelbeghen is some kind of Siberian god or devil."

Stark looked annoyed for a moment, but then his oleaginous façade returned.

"Quite! I'm so glad you've done some background reading. Then you will know that Yelbeghen is commonly shown as a seven-headed dragon. As you can see, the idol in the drawing has been mutilated, losing all its heads. Not to mention its limbs and tail."

Craig looked at the picture again.

"How do you know it's not just a random boulder? How did Sanagi identify the idol?"

Tara pointed at what Craig had thought were just random marks on the stone.

"There's some kind of inscription, though it's very faint."

Stark clapped his hands.

"Excellent! The keen-eyed scientific observer. The inscription gives the game away. The point is that the idol was brought to Japan and became the icon of Sanagi's cult. He was denounced by his religion's leaders and broke away, going underground. They were alleged to have used dark magic to assassinate many people—foreigners and Japanese deemed too Westernized. In all, they were blamed for dozens of deaths over around eight years. But things quieted down after the sixties."

The dealer leaned forward, confiding now.

"Until recently. There has been a rise in occultism in Japan, and with it, a spate of strange occurrences. Deaths caused by paranormal entities. Not just ghosts, but also the *yokai*, creatures of Japanese folklore."

"Like the nine-tailed fox?" Craig asked.

Tara looked surprised.

"I was into anime as a teenager," he confessed. "Fox girls were kind of commonplace."

"It seems you have layers," Stark remarked.

He went on to outline a plan for the mission, but, despite Stark's use of fancy terms, it boiled down to "go to Japan for a few weeks and sniff around". Tara asked if they would get any help from local experts. Stark named a Professor Tanaka in Kyoto as a leading authority on the cult and related matters.

"No ninjas or anything like that?" Craig asked. "I mean, if this cult is still active, they'll outnumber us. And you said they're violent fanatics."

"Yes, but the cult is small, according to my sources," Stark said, "only half a dozen members or so. I'm sure you have the resources to outwit them. Remember, you have extraordinary abilities the cultists might never have encountered. And you have succeeded twice. I have every confidence in your ability to bring home the bacon."

"How much does this particular slice of bacon weigh?" Tara asked.

"I believe the idol is not large," the dealer replied. "One strong man could carry it."

Craig did not ask if he met that criterion because he knew Stark would say of course he did. Stark went on to outline some lines of inquiry. The cult had last been heard of in the north of Japan, so it would make sense to begin searching there. As before, a large sum would be paid in advance, and all expenses paid by Stark. When he named their fee, Craig struggled not to look impressed. It was twice as much as the previous job.

"You're buying this for a collector?" Tara asked. "Like the amulet and the sword?"

"Indeed!" Stark said. "This one is the jackpot, though. The collector in question is very interested in the idol. Just to sweeten the offer, a very large bonus will accrue if you secure it within twenty-eight days. Twice the promised fee."

Craig was about to ask why that specific time when Tara kicked him in the shin. She was right. Stark never answered questions that were so specific. It would be equally pointless to quiz him on the power the idol was supposed to have. Even if he answered, Stark seemed to delight in leaving out crucial facts. Doing their own research would be more reliable, anyway.

"Okay, that's cool. I guess we'd better get ready for a long flight," he said instead.

Stark stood and wished them a pleasant journey. His unctuous charm coupled with his new appearance made him seem like a dodgy realtor. Craig and Tara waited until he got outside to discuss the mission.

"Twenty-eight days is a lunar month," Tara pointed out. "Completing the task in that period presumably has some mystical significance to the creep. I'm not buying this BS about a mysterious collector. Stark wants the thing."

Craig agreed, then asked her what she thought about the man's appearance.

"I'm guessing some kind of enchantment," Tara mused. "There are lots of ways to change your appearance…"

She paused as Craig jerked his head around.

"What is it?" she asked.

One of the ghosts that hung around Hannigan's was even more agitated than before, waving its arms and screeching. What's more, the spirit was bearing down on a young man who'd just crossed the road and was heading for the pub. Craig ran to the door and out onto the sidewalk. The young man stopped, seeing what looked like a crazy and possibly drunken person staring at him. Then, his unseen assailant plunged both hands into his brain.

"No!" Craig grabbed the victim, who was spasming in some kind of seizure, and swung him around to shield him. He felt a searing coldness as the ghost interpenetrated his body. The pain was so intense that he cried out. Tara had taken a couple of seconds to grasp the situation. She helped support the victim.

"Get him inside!" she shouted needlessly.

The ghost made another pass at the hapless stranger before the patrons could get the guy across the threshold. Melody opened the way to the back room where, she told them, Harry kept a first-aid kit. One of the other customers shouted that they had called 911, and a young woman declared that she was a trainee paramedic, which was reassuring.

Craig helped carry the victim into the back and then stepped away. The room was too crowded. He looked out at the street and saw the frantic ghost repeatedly hurling itself against Hannigan's invisible barrier. Then, the thing from above reached down and snatched the deranged spirit away.

Craig thought back on the lightning-fast encounter. The ghost had been ranting and shrieking, and most of what it said made no sense. But one thing stuck in Craig's mind. The ghost had looked him in the eye and, for that one moment, spoken with apparent sanity.

"The time of fire is coming."

Chapter 7
Discussions with the Dead

"Time of fire, huh?"

It was early evening. Jeopardy had finished, and Billy was willing to discuss the current situation. Chloe was nowhere to be seen, but might, in theory, be listening. Craig was sitting next to Billy and drinking a cool beer. It might not be entirely wise given his recent exertions, but he felt like he needed it.

"Yeah," Craig said. "Just another one of the crazies going on about the end of the world."

Billy got up off the sofa and stretched. How the ghost could sit in the first place, and why he would need to stretch, baffled Craig. When he'd asked, Billy simply said, "You spend enough time dead, you learn a few tricks." Craig had asked Chloe, and she had been puzzled, too. Ask any ghost how they could walk through walls but stood on the floor without difficulty, and they resorted to evasion or doubletalk.

"End of the world," Billy mused. "I wonder if it's that simple."

He stopped stretching and looked enviously at the beer in Craig's hand. That was one thing no ghost could enjoy, as far as Craig knew.

"Simple?" Craig said. "The end of the world?"

Billy pointed out of the window.

"That world out there could end anytime; you know that. Some lunatic dictator or a stressed-out military type pushing the wrong button. Somebody sees a blip on a screen and decides it's time for World War III. And that's before we get onto Mother Nature's little surprises like coronal mass ejections. One of those could wipe out the whole internet and most of the power grid in a few hours."

Craig felt his mind boggling, and then he remembered that Billy liked to watch the Discovery Channel and often surfed the web when Craig was out.

"So, what's your point? We might as well give up because we're all doomed?"

Billy folded his arms and glowered at him.

"No, dumbass. I'm saying the exact opposite! It's not the end of the world you should be scared of. It's the danger of a new world order."

Craig wondered if he was about to get a dose of conspiracy theories. Seeing his expression, Billy frowned balefully, half-turned, and pointed to the faded tattoo on his arm. The seven-headed dragon.

"No, I don't mean all that conspiracy bullshit, I mean a world transformed by Yelbeghen and his disciples. It's not the people who want to blow it all up that you should be scared of, buddy. It's the bastards who want to build something big regardless of who gets hurt. The ones who want to create a new world that doesn't have you in it."

Craig thought of the new-look Peregrine Stark in his designer clothes. Was that man preparing for a world remade in the image of a strange deity? It seemed absurd that the middleman would be the trigger for something immense and terrifying, but Craig had glimpsed strange things when moving people on. Heavens and hells existed. What if somebody wanted to create a heaven on earth for themselves that would be hell for others?

Billy talked on about history, and how clever men without principles had made most of it. Craig finished his beer and got another from the fridge. He was halfway through the second bottle when Billy ran out of steam. The biker fell silent, which seemed to be Chloe's cue. The emo girl appeared by the door of the apartment, her eyes downcast.

"The wanderer returns!" Billy proclaimed and glanced at Craig. "Well, guess I'd better go and see what the word is on the street."

Billy vanished, leaving Craig smiling. Billy was tactful in a heavy-handed way. Chloe seemed even shyer than usual, and that usually meant some personal revelation was in the offing. Craig waited silently. Chloe eventually looked at him, but only for a moment. The smears of makeup that could never be fixed gave her a tragic, waif-like appearance.

"Billy's right." She moved slowly to the sofa. "Things are bad. A lot of the others say Yelbeghen is coming. Some say he will be a liberator. Kind of."

Craig was puzzled.

"Liberator? You mean, liberating ghosts?"

Chloe nodded.

"From their captivity on this plane of existence. I don't know how, but there's talk of this dark god, Yelbeghen, breaking all the barriers between worlds. Letting the dead back into the world of the living, maybe. I can't be sure, though, because I get scared when other ghosts talk crazy, so I kind of avoid them."

"Very wise."

Craig gestured to the place Billy had left vacant. Instead of sitting by him, the ghost perched on the arm of the sofa.

"Is there something else?" he asked.

She met his gaze for a second time and then resumed staring at her spectral Doc Martens. When she spoke, it was just above a whisper.

"Before you go away I... I want to go see my grandmother. I miss her. She kind of raised me, and I wasn't grateful enough and ran away to do dumb things, and then I died and couldn't get to her and tell her I'm sorry because she lived too far away, and then... then she died and... I want to see her..."

Craig got up and braced himself. He wanted to ask her to wait, explain that maybe in another day or so, he'd have fully recovered. He didn't have to leave for Japan for four days. But perhaps he didn't have one day. Maybe nobody did, thinking back to what Billy had said. If he was going to do right by his friend, he would do it now. As sacrifices went, it was a small one.

"It's okay," he said. "I'm sure she wants to see you, too."

"I guess," the ghost said.

Then Chloe looked him in the eye for the third time.

"Every time you go away, I think you won't come back, so I don't want to be here…"

"I get it," he said quietly. "And I'm sorry I have to go."

It was, as always, easier with a willing subject. Chloe stood facing Craig as he concentrated on opening the portal above them. This time, the whirlpool of light appeared in a few seconds and grew rapidly. On the other side of the vortex was darkness, which puzzled him at first. Then he felt trepidation. Was Chloe, kind and gentle Chloe, destined for a bleak afterlife?

Then, a thin sliver of yellow-white light appeared, and Craig realized he was watching a door open into a darkened room. A silhouette appeared, and then a slender woman with bobbed dark hair walked in.

"You were just having a bad dream." The woman sat on the bed. Her voice was gentle, with just a hint of weariness. "Don't be scared; dreams can't hurt you. Come here, let Grandma give you a hug."

Chloe was rising toward the portal, her arms upraised, and her expression one of yearning. At the last moment, the ghost looked down at Craig and smiled, then mouthed the words, "Thank you". A sense of warmth washed over him as the vortex grew brighter, blazing with blue-white radiance. Craig was suddenly flooded with Chloe's memories—a childhood marked by neglect, fear, and loneliness, but also love and security like flashes of sun through rain. The essence of a person's being was not a simple narrative; he knew that. But this was a deluge of emotion jumbled with intense snatches of experience. A bleak Christmas morning vied for his attention with the scent of peach cobbler and the pangs of adolescent love. A life, even a tragically brief one, is overwhelming when experienced all at once.

Then, Craig saw himself as she had seen him. A kind man, a little goofy, and a bit of a lost soul. But somehow taller and better-looking than he had ever thought himself to be. Not quite an ideal man but better in some ways. A man who could be trusted, perhaps even loved, had things been different.

"Take care."

Her final words. Selfless and kind. Then, he was slumped on the couch, blinking and tearful, alone in his apartment. The exhaustion of moving Chloe on was trivial compared to what felt very much like a sense of bereavement.

His journey had not even begun, but already he had lost a friend.

CHAPTER 8
LIKE A BAT OUT OF HELL

Chloe left on Monday. Tara picked up Craig at his place bright and early on Thursday morning, and they were soon on the interstate. Their first destination was the store of Felicia Clovis, a discreet dealer in paranormal items. Along the way, Craig remained alert for possible attacks, ghostly or otherwise. But nothing unusual had happened by the time they pulled up outside the store.

This time, they had arrived before Shane, as there was no sign of his car. They got out, with Craig groaning in relief and stretching. Then, he looked up at the storefront. Something was different. The name? No, it was still *F. Clovis, Dealer in Unusual Items*. But the typeface seemed changed. Hadn't it been gold Gothic script on a black background? Now, the letters were silver on dark blue.

"Yeah," Tara said when he asked about this. "I don't know how she does it, but the façade revamps itself every few months. When I first met her, the store had an art deco look. I asked her about it, but she just said she employs very discreet people."

"Maybe they're not people." Craig lingered to study the display in the large window.

"Maybe," Tara concurred, standing beside him.

The items in the window were an eclectic mixture of touristy stuff and odd, sometimes baffling objects. Books purporting to be grimoires rubbed shoulders with charms and amulets. There was also a glass apparatus that looked like a medieval chemistry set. A large plastic doll lay slumped in one corner, wearing a cute dress but devoid of hair. It had huge, black eyes with no whites. In the opposite corner was a small wooden cabinet, its door open, and the interior marked with what looked like astrological symbols. Craig leaned forward to peer into the shadowy interior. The symbols swam and rearranged themselves on the wooden panels, and the door swung open a little wider. Craig flinched and took a step back.

"Yeah, I think that's a spirit cabinet," Tara said. "You don't see many these days. Most are in museums, I guess, or private collections. Very expensive, some kind of special commission."

"But there are no price tags," he pointed out.

"If you have to ask how much it costs, you can't afford it," Tara said. "Come on, we're expected. She's probably brewing a pot of tea right now."

Tara was proved wrong as soon as they walked inside. Felicia Clovis was standing and talking to a middle-aged woman who—to Craig's surprise—had a stroller with the bonnet pulled down. The stroller seemed wildly incongruous in the store. Felicia Clovis glanced over at them.

"I'll be with you shortly. Feel free to browse."

Clearly, the dealer didn't want to acknowledge their association in front of this customer. The woman with the stroller looked at the newcomers. She had a hard, lined face, with thin lips and small, deep-set eyes that reminded Craig of metal studs. The woman turned back to Felicia and started speaking in a low voice. Craig, conflicted about eavesdropping, drifted down one aisle, examining jars of straw-colored fluid that obscured their contents. He was quite glad of that when he read some of the labels.

"I appreciate that, but you must understand my position."

Felicia had raised her voice. The dealer sounded impatient and keen to be rid of the stroller woman. The latter said something Craig couldn't hear. She sounded ticked off as well. He peeked between two jars to see the woman folding back the black bonnet on the stroller. Felicia shook her head and crossed her arms. Craig could not see the stroller's occupant from his angle, but then, a small head came into view. He gasped. Could an ordinary child be so hairy? And those ears, like a fox. Or maybe a bat?

46

Then, the head turned one-hundred-and-eighty degrees, and Craig looked into a tiny old man's face, contorted in anger. The thing in the stroller screeched and leaped up. Craig lost sight of it, thanks to his limited viewpoint, but he got the distinct impression of big, leathery wings being spread.

Tara shrieked.

They ran down the aisle toward the front of the shop. The bat thing was flapping about the store, its leathery pinions knocking items off shelves and sending the old-fashioned light fittings swinging wildly. The woman customer was shouting something in a language Craig didn't recognize. Felicia had retreated behind her cash desk and was jabbing fingers at the flying creature. Her lips were moving, but she was making no audible sounds.

The small monster swooped at Craig. He realized he had nothing to contribute to the situation but panic. Sharp claws raked the top of his head as he ducked. Then, he felt something warm and wet splatter onto the back of his neck, accompanied by a foul stink.

It just crapped on me, he thought. *What the hell?*

He rolled under a table just as the thing swooped again. A stink of formaldehyde vied with the odor of the bat thing's excrement. Craig saw a shattered jar a quarter-full with cloudy, yellow fluid. Something was climbing out of it. It was a hand, black and shriveled and severed at the wrist, but so lively that Craig almost laughed.

It occurred to him that the hand shouldn't be allowed to wander off, so he reached out and grabbed it. There was a brief struggle, and the feel of the leathery flesh was disgusting, but he pinned down the wriggling hand.

Goddamn nightmare, he thought, peeking out from under the table. A hideous upside-down face appeared, staring down at him.

The bat creature gave a deranged shriek of fury and leaped onto the floor. Craig shuffled away on his butt and kicked at the nightmarish visage.

Easily dodging the kick, the beast launched itself at Craig, its jaws wide and drooling. It had barely gotten airborne before Tara's jacket appeared, intercepting the weird beast. The garment acted like a living thing, wrapping itself around its quarry. There was a muffled squawk and a thud as the trapped creature fell to the floor. The hard-faced woman rushed forward, as Felicia shouted something that Craig took a second to process.

"Control your offspring!"

The woman pulled the jacket off the small monster and picked it up, hugging it close to her and kissing the top of its hirsute head. The bat thing chittered some more, and Craig saw that one of its wings was hanging limply while the other was folded up against its body.

"Never mind, my darling, never mind. We'll make it better," the woman crooned.

It's her child, Craig thought. *But it can't be. It's not human. Oh, God.*

"I've got a first-aid kit." Felicia was businesslike now and standing over the mother and infant. "We can put a splint on that wing, and I have a salve for the pain."

Then, turning to Craig, she added: "Maybe you'd better wait in the office. Both of you."

He held out the severed hand, which Felicia took without a hint of surprise.

"Thanks very much. I'll lock it in a drawer for now."

As he walked past the nameless woman, she gave him a look that could have curdled milk. The bat thing raised its head and glared at him, gibbering some more. The creature's eyes were huge, golden orbs that might have been beautiful on another kind of face. As it was, they contrasted with the ears, not to mention the pointed muzzle full of sharp teeth.

"What did I do?" he mumbled.

"You… spoil… everything!" the little monster spat in a grating, high-pitched voice.

48

Jeez, he thought, averting his eyes. *Give me a break.*

CHAPTER 9

A HALF-FORGOTTEN PROPHET

"What the hell did the bat mean, I 'spoil everything'?"

Tara didn't answer. Instead, she reached into her bag and took out a tissue.

"Turn around; I'll wipe most of the crap off. Wow, it stinks to high heaven!"

Craig did as he was bidden.

They were in the small back room of Felicia's store. There had been no more disturbances, so presumably, getting Craig out of reach of the bat creature had calmed it down. The scratches it had left on his scalp still stung, and the excrement it had pooped onto him was filling the small room with a very pungent odor.

"There, I think I got most of it off," Tara said after a minute of wiping and dabbing, "but a shower would be a good idea. Felicia wouldn't mind, I'm sure. Bathroom's through there."

She nodded to a second door Craig hadn't noticed during his last visit. It was almost hidden by a large bookcase.

"If you're sure…"

"Go. Be less stinky," Tara insisted.

"I mean, I know I don't go to many parties," Craig continued, "but I don't spoil everything, do I? What the hell does that even mean?"

"Stop obsessing about it, and I might call you stunningly handsome and charismatic," Tara observed wryly. "But first, go and take a damn shower!"

She walked over to a small table where, as predicted, a kettle and teapot were set out next to some cups. There was also a large chocolate cake under a glass cover. Craig sensed that he might miss out if he wasn't quick, and entered the bathroom.

He emerged fifteen minutes later, feeling fragrant, as he'd used Felicia's shampoo and body wash. The shopkeeper was sitting at her desk sipping tea while Tara perched on the edge of a small sofa and indulged herself in what looked like a second slice of cake.

"Ah, here he is, right as rain!" Felicia exclaimed. "Do pour yourself a cuppa, you poor thing. I wish I'd never seen that ghastly woman and her demon spawn. It will take me ages to clean up properly. I've dealt with the worst of it, though. Say what you like about magic, but there's nothing like an honest mop and bucket in a crisis."

"I'd like to help," Craig said seriously. "I mean, I don't know why, but it looks like I triggered that attack somehow."

Felicia made a deprecatory gesture.

"Oh, you are too kind, but there's no need. The damage is mostly superficial, apart from one preserved organ that has already spoiled. I added it to her bill."

Craig poured some tea and, wielding a large cake knife, cut himself a generous portion. Then, he sat next to Tara.

"So, that thing… it was the result of her… I mean, with a demon? I don't get it. What's the upside?"

Felicia smiled at his expression. Craig flushed, feeling like a prude.

"I'm afraid a lot of people feel there is an upside, or several," the Englishwoman said. "Firstly, the sex can be marvelous, or so I'm told! Sordid, I know, but it's true. There's no accounting for taste, especially in the bedroom. Or on a trapeze, or wherever. Some demons are… well, let's say they have many interesting attributes and do not lack stamina. Second, a woman who aspires to give birth but is unable to do so with a human male can still be impregnated by a demon, as was the case with that client. She left it a little late in life."

Craig struggled to make sense of that explanation. The thought that the desire to give birth would lead anyone down such a convoluted path dismayed him. Yet, he felt he was somehow the one at fault for not understanding enough.

"Okay," he sighed, "but why did it attack me? And…"

He hesitated as Tara gave him a warning look, then spoke to the dealer.

"He's getting a bit fixated on what Bat Boy said."

Felicia's expression became serious, and she frowned slightly.

"That, I admit, is puzzling. According to the mother, her precious offspring can sense a person's destiny. She came to me because she wants me to help train the creature. Hone its talents. But I gave up offering private tuition a long time ago, for humans or anyone else."

Craig had a sudden, surreal vision of Felicia standing in front of a classroom of tiny horrors. While his mind was quietly boggling, Tara spoke through a mouthful of cake.

"Any idea why Craig was singled out?"

"Possibly. You know, something about that seems familiar."

Felicia thought for a few moments and then got up and went to a bookshelf. The volume she took down was slim, with dog-eared black covers and a slightly torn spine. The dealer paced in front of her guests, flipping through pages.

"I'm sure I read something not long ago… ah, yes, this might be it."

She looked at Craig and smiled.

"This is an obscure book by an equally obscure gentleman, one Thaddeus Crutchley. He claimed to be a prophet. It was privately printed in London in 1822. Crutchley never won much of a following, but he was notorious for falling into trances and giving out obscure predictions."

"Like Nostradamus?" Craig asked.

Felicia smiled.

"If you ordered your Nostradamus from Wish, perhaps. Listen to this."

Felicia stopped pacing and adopted a more formal tone.

"'Two centuries and more will pass, and a seer who is a seeker will be marked by the spawn of evil. This man's power will be great, for he will hasten the dead to their final reckoning.' That sort of fits the situation, doesn't it?"

"It's a little vague," Tara commented. "It could be Craig, but maybe there are other seers? Evil does a hell of a lot of spawning."

"Yeah," Craig chimed in, "isn't there anything else? I don't want to spoil anything, let alone everything."

Felicia hesitated, and then they heard the tinkle of the bell above the shop door. Felicia gave a brisk apology and hurried out, taking the book with her. She reappeared a few moments later, looking worried. Shane Ryan was right behind her.

"Step away from the teacups, guys," he said. "Things could get messy any minute."

The others were already standing.

"What's up?" Tara asked.

"Some shady characters trying to look inconspicuous," Shane replied. "That always stands out. They're in an SUV with tinted windows. I caught sight of a ghost moving around back."

He turned to Felicia, who was working on her PC. Craig assumed she was checking security cameras.

"Ghosts and other bogies can't get in without my permission," she said without looking up. "I have good defenses against regular humans, too..."

She hesitated.

"Could that bat thing have damaged any of your barriers?" Tara asked urgently.

"I don't think so," Felicia replied. "Ah, yes, I see them. They're getting out. No sign of anything unusual, but—"

Whatever she was about to say was drowned out by a tremendous noise like a clap of thunder that set Craig's ears ringing. Behind Felicia, a ghostly face appeared out of the wall, smiling cruelly. Long, wiry arms reached out, with fingers seeking to plunge themselves into the woman's brain.

CHAPTER 10

ONSLAUGHT

Craig felt sure he was too late, even as he ran toward Felicia. Her eyeballs rolled up, and her facial muscles became slack as the ghost hands worked viciously inside her skull. Ghosts could do tremendous damage to a living person in no time. Whatever wards and barriers Felicia had established had failed.

The ghost pulled its fingers from the woman's skull and grinned at Craig as Felicia slumped to the floor. It was, Craig saw now, a man who'd been quite elderly when he died. He had a debauched face that was sly and full of malice. This was a being who enjoyed making others suffer.

Craig lashed out, his fist passing through the ghost's face. It was a futile attempt at a blow that sent stinging needles of pain into his hand. The killer ghost leered and then darted forward, jabbing his fingers into Craig's eye sockets. The pain was immense, and the impact blinded him. Cursing, he flailed and then hurled himself backward. He collided with someone and heard Tara curse. Then, he could see again, and the ghost was frozen, his mouth open in an "O" of astonishment.

Tara's iron brooch emerged from the phantom's chest. It vanished, leaving behind a howl of anger and frustration. Blinking back tears, Craig knelt by Felicia, hoping that she might still be alive.

"Call 911!" he yelled.

"No time!"

That was Shane, standing in the doorway, throwing punches at an assailant Craig could not see. Then, the Marine was thrown back into the room, and the attacker appeared. Craig gasped. It was not a ghost, or at least not in the conventional sense. In form, it was somewhere between a man and an ape, with a huge barrel chest, enormous shoulders, and huge, muscular arms. The legs were short and bowed with massive, splayed feet. It was naked but covered in a thick layer of hair.

Shane threw another punch, and the thing's head was jolted back on its shoulders. It seemed to have no neck. Its small, deep-set eyes widened, and it snarled, revealing huge canines. Shane kept landing blows, but they didn't bother his opponent much. It raised a colossal arm and tried to deliver a wide, roundhouse punch to Shane. Experienced and agile, Shane ducked and dodged. But it was a small room, and the ape thing was backing him up against a bookcase.

Craig looked around for a weapon. There was a heavy brass paperweight in the shape of a Buddha on Felicia's desk. He picked it up. The ape thing noticed and was distracted for a moment.

The distraction enabled Shane to deliver a series of vicious punches to the entity's head. The intensity of the attack knocked the grotesque spirit off-balance. It roared in anger and confusion, shaking its head and waving its overly long arms to ward off Shane's attack.

Craig grabbed his jacket and took out an iron dagger, preparing to hurl it. But then, he hesitated. A third intruder had appeared. A young man with rose-tinted glasses was leveling a gun at Shane, who was preoccupied with his hefty opponent.

"Look out!" Craig flung the dagger at this new target with clumsy haste. The gunman might have been put off by the shouted warning. He fired, but his shot went wide and high, shattering the front of a glass display cabinet. Craig's dagger, spinning wildly, struck the man's head with a glancing blow with the hilt. He staggered to one side but recovered and took aim at Craig.

For a split second, the universe seemed to consist of a blue-black circle of metal. There was no way the guy could miss. Craig flinched, closed his eyes, and threw up his hands, knowing it was futile, waiting for the shot.

It didn't come. Instead, when Craig looked again, the man in the tinted glasses was falling sideways onto Felicia's Axminster carpet.

Felicia's ghost was standing where the gunman had stood, smiling ruefully at Craig. She mouthed two words at Craig and then raised a hand and waved goodbye. Then she was gone. Craig had no time to think about what had happened.

Shane was still at it with the ape-ghost. He managed to get his hands on the animal's head and crushed it until the spirit exploded. They were all thrown backward by the blast, but were otherwise alright.

"That was close." Tara got up and bent forward to rest her hands on her legs.

"No time," Shane grated. "There's still someone in the car. We need to deal with whoever it is."

Craig started to protest, but Shane strode past him without a glance. He grasped what the man meant. It made sense to deal with an enemy when you knew their location.

"Back us up." Tara patted him on the arm as she hurried after Shane. "But don't be a hero."

The man Felicia had killed was halfway blocking the doorway. Craig stooped to pick up his gun, surprised by its weight. He knew he was no marksman and kept his finger off the trigger. He'd fired a gun on a shooting range many years earlier, but holding the weapon was a definite confidence booster. As he followed the others, he pointed the pistol at the ceiling, aware of the risk he presented to his friends.

The ghost that had killed Felicia reappeared just inside the shop doorway. It charged at Shane but showed no real grasp of tactics. This time, Shane easily destroyed the elderly ghost. The others were more prepared and shielded themselves from the explosion.

Shane had not had enough time to recover when another ape-ghost appeared, looking angrier than the first one. Once more, the ghost hunter managed to dodge and weave, landing a few stunning blows before dancing back toward Felicia's cash desk. Craig, still holding the gun vertically, looked past the fray toward the SUV with tinted windows a stone's throw from the store. There was no sign of activity in or near it.

Tara, meanwhile, set her flying daggers whirling toward the huge, unwieldy attacker. Shane seized the moment of confusion to move closer to his opponent and land more blows, but the ghost had anticipated this and charged forward, its enormous arms outstretched.

Shane spotted the danger a moment too late. He only hit the entity once before he was crushed against the ghost's chest. It lifted Shane and swung him around as a shield against the flying blades. Craig knew that he and Tara could not free Shane by force. Those massive arms were too strong.

Shane was being crushed to death.

CHAPTER 11

CONTACT LOST

Craig ran forward, determined to save Shane. Tara shouted a warning that he ignored and placed his hands on the enormous, misshapen head. The ghost felt solid, all its brute power concentrated in materializing so it could squeeze the life from its opponent. The hairy scalp was cold to the touch, but Craig ignored it.

The ape creature seemed confused by Craig's approach. It bared its fangs. Craig ignored the threat and focused on making contact. It was surprisingly easy to begin the process, perhaps because this being was unburdened by complex thoughts and feelings. Craig felt a portal opening right away and looked up to see something new. Instead of a swirling vortex of light, a patch of blue sky appeared, ragged at the edges.

Move on, Craig urged, trying to control his anxiety and stay focused. *Move on.*

He heard Shane cursing and realized that the other man could at least get air into his lungs. Then, the patch of sky darkened into a starry night with a thin sliver of moon. Craig began to sense the ghost's memories, a mixture of intense sensations from a world long past.

In death, the ape creature had been bound to a small, crudely carved bone that had been some kind of talisman among its kind. He saw the long-dead spirit wandering an unfamiliar landscape, haunting a quiet valley for millennia, baffled, and driven half-crazy by isolation. It yearned for an afterlife it vaguely sensed being held perpetually out of reach. Its kind passed away to be replaced by small, hairless beings who regarded it as a bogeyman that terrorized lone travelers or lurked on the edge of the firelight.

Craig saw the human race through the eyes of a being on the shadowy margin of humankind. A creature that had been commonplace in its time became a legend. All the being's memories were shot through with a nearly overwhelming loneliness. It ended when the bone was discovered, carried away, and placed in a museum.

At first, the ancient spirit was too frightened by these changes to do anything. One day, a fat, grinning man arrived and examined the talisman. This stranger, a telepath, offered the ghost the chance to escape its exile. All it had to do was kill some of the pathetic little humans who infested the world.

This was all made clear to Craig in an instant. His mind reeled at the scale of the ghost's existence, the contrast between its simple nature and the world it was forced to serve in. Then, a surge of anger ended the link between them. The ape creature lashed out, and a massive fist punched Craig in the chest. He was knocked to the floor, but the distraction served its purpose. Shane broke free and delivered another rapid-fire series of punches.

Instead of fighting on, the ghost simply faded, merging with the shadows of the subtly lit store. Tara ran to the doorway to report that the SUV was driving off.

"No way," Shane snapped. "We can't let them get away."

"Are you sure you're okay?" Craig asked.

"No ribs broken, thanks to you," the Marine replied. "Cool trick, but maybe don't try it too often."

"I'll keep that in mind."

They took both cars, with Shane in the lead. He talked to Craig via speakerphone while Tara did her best to keep up. At first, Craig assumed things would be like a cop show, with the prey subtly trying to shake them off. But within minutes, the SUV driver made it clear he was not interested in traffic regulations. He veered wildly across lanes, overtaking recklessly, and terrorizing other drivers. As a result, the pursuers were accompanied by the blaring of horns and frequent tire screeches as they headed for the interstate.

"This is going to get somebody killed," Craig said. "Maybe we should ease off."

"No," Shane replied tersely. "Think how many people these scumbags might kill if we don't deal with them."

Craig looked at his phone. He could not argue with such logic, but another point occurred to him. He tried to frame his argument so that it would not sound like a criticism of Shane. The last thing he wanted was to call the man a hothead.

"Yeah, but if the cops get involved, it could blow the whole mission."

There was a pause, punctuated by another near collision up ahead. A small, white pickup truck had skipped off the road and had one wheel in a drainage ditch. Fortunately, Felicia's store was on the edge of a small town. In a big city, this chase would probably have led to injury or death already, Craig thought.

"You're right," Shane said, adding a few choice curses.

Craig saw Shane's car falling behind the SUV, which was still powering toward the interstate at an insane speed. Tara slowed, and they decided to stop somewhere and hold a council of war. Finding a place to pull over proved tricky, however. More cursing ensued.

Craig suddenly felt very tired. He leaned back and closed his eyes. He heard the pitch of the engine noise and tires changing. Behind his eyelids, he saw familiar green and orange swirls. Phosphenes. Things he'd been seeing since childhood. He'd Googled the subject once and found that scientists disagreed over what caused the glowing patterns. He'd always found them relaxing.

"You okay?" Tara asked.

"Sure. Just kind of beat. I wish—"

Craig hesitated as he noticed something odd about the swirls of light.

They were forming a pattern. A moment later, it was a moving image, distorted but still recognizable. There were vehicles in front, with buildings passing to either side. He was seeing the road they were traveling on.

He opened his eyes. The road ahead was different than the one he'd just seen, projected onto his eyelids. He closed his eyes again.

"What is it?" Tara asked.

"I'm not sure," he replied. "I think…"

The vision appeared again, but fainter. He got a glimpse of someone sitting at the wheel of a car and felt a brief sting of emotion. It was dislike, resentment, a desire to harm, and frustration at being bound by powerful magic. Then, the weird internal movie fragmented, and there was nothing but the familiar, meaningless filaments of light.

"I think I just contacted the mind of the ape ghost," he said. "Just for a second. But it was real, I'm sure. I didn't imagine it."

A few minutes later, they were in a Costco parking lot. Craig explained what had happened as best he could. Shane was predictably disappointed that they couldn't track the enemy to their lair but intrigued by the new twist on Craig's power. Tara seemed more thoughtful; anxious, even.

"If you're linked to that thing, who's to say the ones controlling it won't be able to track us via your perceptions?"

Craig had already mulled that one over.

"Well, I got no sense that our ape guy knew I was in his head," he said, "It seems like we're being tracked, anyway. There must be a dozen ways those guys—whoever they are—could do that."

Shane gave him a hard stare but didn't disagree. Tara spoke.

"We need to get to Japan and put an end to all this, one way or another."

She reached into her jacket and took out a small, dog-eared book without a dustcover. Craig recognized it as the one Felicia had read from less than an hour ago.

"Yeah, I pinched it on impulse," Tara confirmed. "You never know when a set of two-hundred-year-old prophecies from a guy called Crutchley might come in handy."

CHAPTER 12

ABOVE THE CLOUDS

The nonstop flight from Boston to Tokyo would take thirteen hours and change. It looked easier on a screen, but now that Craig was experiencing it, he thought he might go a little stir-crazy. He didn't like flying. He told himself this was because of the confinement, boredom, and recycled air. But deep down, he knew it was a more basic fear. The fear of being at a ludicrous altitude in a pressurized metal and plastic tube. A tube hurtling through the stratosphere under the impetus of engines that might conk out, catch fire, or drop off.

Statistically, crossing the road is far more dangerous, he told himself for the umpteenth time. *And so is changing a light bulb.*

The plane dipped suddenly, then leveled out with a slight bump. Someone gave a little shriek, and then there was some nervous laughter.

"Just turbulence; nothing to worry about," a flight attendant said as she passed. "Just a little bump. Everybody can relax!"

Craig had downloaded a popular audiobook about Japan onto his phone but couldn't concentrate for more than a few minutes at a time. He had gleaned that Japanese people were very polite and helpful but averse to small talk; efficient but sometimes inflexible. Shy and solitary folk, by and large, who didn't want to stand out from the crowd.

That sounded okay to Craig. Maybe he'd been Japanese in a previous existence. But if so, he had retained zero grasp of the language. The book offered useful words and phrases that he mouthed under his breath. *Kon'nichiwa. Sumimasen. Arigato gozaimasu.* After a while, he felt he might be able to order a coffee without making a fool of himself.

The narrator moved on to emergencies, and the importance of downloading a phone app that alerted you to impending disasters. Craig listened to descriptions of earthquakes, tsunamis, and nuclear accidents. Oh, and Mount Fuji, on the outskirts of Tokyo, was classed by geologists as an active volcano. Fujiyama was long overdue for a major eruption. He tried to absorb information on where to shelter. High ground or a tall building for a tsunami. Open spaces for an earthquake. Volcanic eruption—better to just be somewhere else.

There had been two notable earthquakes already this century and Japan—like California—was overdue for a big one. It was weird that a society constantly under threat of natural disasters should be so calm and collected. But then, Craig reflected, perhaps that was the key. If people weren't cool-headed and responsible, the whole place would fall apart.

That might be why violent crime was almost nonexistent, even in big cities. Japan was still a cash-based society, in part because theft and burglary were so rare. The trains and other public transport were renowned for their punctuality. If a train was late, the railroad company issued certificates to commuters to prove they couldn't help being late for work. Craig tried to imagine any American company admitting responsibility for any failure, let alone putting it in writing. He felt like he was learning about a parallel universe, a world so complex he could not grasp even the basics.

But this might, he felt, be due to his fatigue. Craig's normal routine had been shot to hell.

He opened his eyes and checked the audiobook's content listings. There was a whole chapter on religion, folklore, and mythology that could be useful. He jumped to it, and soon learned that, as well as regular ghosts, Japan had many supernatural beings. Some were demons called *oni*, but others, known as *yokai*, might be harmless or even helpful.

Many *yokai* were shapeshifters and some could assume any form. There were the legendary nine-tailed foxes who often took on a human guise. Such fox beings were seductive and sometimes benevolent. But, perhaps inevitably, the book focused more on the dangerous entities, of which there was a bewildering array. He listened to accounts of snow vampires, slit-mouthed women, and several varieties of giant spiders. All the giant spiders seemed to be shapeshifters, just for good measure.

Craig stopped listening. He had absorbed some information, such as how to say "hello" and "thank you". He knew there was an ever-present threat of widespread disaster. And he was now aware of a whole array of weird and often deadly creatures that he'd not known existed. That was more than enough research for now.

Craig felt he should at least doze, but sleeping had become an issue. Shane and Tara said staying awake made more sense, and fended off jetlag. They had been mainlining strong coffee before and during the flight. Craig had tried to emulate them, but now, he felt that if another caffeine molecule entered his system, he might start bounding around the cabin.

Next to him, Tara was chuckling at an in-flight movie Craig had seen and not liked much. Beyond Tara, in the aisle seat, Shane was sipping another cup of extra-strength coffee. Craig looked past his companions, to the people across the aisle. They were Asian, possibly Japanese, and might be middle-aged or a little older. The man wore an eye mask and had reclined his seat. The woman was looking out her window, presumably at the sea of clouds that obscured the land. Craig looked out his window again and saw the shadow of their Boeing, vast and distorted.

Craig's eyelids were too heavy. No amount of coffee could keep a man awake. The seat felt wonderfully comfortable. The background noise of conversation and assorted technologies blurred and faded. Strange words and phrases vied for his attention. *Pachinko. Yakuza. Kawaii.* He woke to find Tara nudging him.

"You're drooling," she said with a grin. "Just thought you'd like to know."

Craig mumbled a thank you and wiped the trickle of saliva from his chin. The cabin lights had been dimmed, with only a few spots of brightness showing here and there. He looked out of the window and saw nothing but night. How long had he been asleep?

His reflected face looked a little pale and flabby, and his eyes were dull. Behind him, he saw Tara sitting up and gazing over his shoulder.

"Gawd, you look awful, mate," she said in a faux British accent. "Seriously, I can't believe I nearly let you shag me."

Craig turned to see her smirking unpleasantly.

"Oh, come on, Craig," she went on, dropping the accent. "You think I'd let a loser like you do the wild thing? I'm out of your league. You're cute, but so pathetic, always the victim, always worrying, never manning up and just getting it done. But it was fun seeing you panting like an ugly little puppy dog hoping for a treat."

Craig's initial confusion lasted for another second.

"Oh, this is a dream," he said. "I get it. Anxiety and stuff."

Tara leaned closer, and her features seemed to flow, losing definition. When she spoke again, it was in a low, harsh voice.

"Just because it's a dream doesn't mean I can't hurt you, asshole!"

Her eyes glowed a lurid yellow, and her mouth opened to show a row of razor-sharp fangs. Then a black, pointed tongue shot out, just missing his right eye. He tried to fight off the demon, but it was too strong. It pinned him against the window, and the vicious tongue raked against his cheek, its texture like shark skin.

"Kissy kissy, Kermie!" chortled the thing that had been Tara.

He yelled and woke to the real Tara shaking him by the shoulder. A flight attendant appeared, smiling professionally but looking anxious. Shane spoke quietly to her. Craig heard the words "nervous flyer" and "insomnia". The young woman relaxed and chatted more with Shane. Meanwhile, Tara patted Craig's hand and asked him about his nightmare.

"It was some kind of—entity." He tactfully decided not to mention any details. "Thanks. Maybe Shane was right about staying awake."

The attendant left. Craig and Tara talked some more. Conversation flagged, and Craig dozed off again. He woke to find Tara thumbing through the book she had retrieved from Felicia's collection. She looked up.

"Maybe getting some shuteye isn't a bad idea," she said sympathetically. "I know you hate flying. If I stumble across anything interesting in this…"

She waggled the ancient book at him.

"I'll wake you up, promise."

Craig smiled.

"Thanks. But if it's anything like, 'He will be killed by a giant spider,' don't tell me."

"What?" asked Tara, puzzled.

"Nothing," he assured her. "I'll get that shuteye."

He leaned back and then turned to face the window. His eyelids felt heavy as lead. *This time,* he told himself, *there'll be no nightmares. No dreams at all.*

Craig was jolted awake without knowing he had fallen asleep. They had hit more turbulence. The cabin lights flickered for a moment, and he had the horrible conviction that the plane's systems were failing. His stomach lurched as if he was plunging downward on a roller coaster. He looked out of the window and saw the great expanse of cloud below them. In the distance, columns of vapor seemed to erupt from the cloud base.

"Please remain calm," came the announcement. "This is just another patch of turbulence."

The cabin lights flickered again and then shone steadily. Someone swore in a row behind Craig. A child was crying somewhere. The plane banked and turned, and Craig could no longer see the enormous cloud pillars.

"Another rude awakening, huh?" Tara said.

Craig did not reply for a moment.

"You okay?" she asked.

"Yeah," he said. "I just… I didn't have time to count them all."

Tara made an interrogative noise.

"But I think," he said, "that there were seven."

CHAPTER 13
ONE IN A MILLION GHOSTS

"This is the best airport I've ever seen," Craig said. "It's so clean and quiet."

"How many airports have you seen, just for information?" Shane asked.

"Well, this is the fourth, but the point stands."

Narita Airport was remarkable for its air of smooth, calm efficiency. There were so many staff on hand, and they all seemed keen to be helpful. Craig watched in amazement at the luggage carousel as a handful of uniformed men turned the cases around as they came into view, making sure that the handles faced outward.

"I mean, look at those guys. That's an actual job!"

"Different culture," Tara said. "But there are always downsides. When I was here for a conference, I thought I was in some kind of Utopia. Everything was clean and efficient, and everybody was very polite and smiling. Then I tried speaking English to people and realized most Japanese can't understand more than a few words."

Craig remembered what he'd learned from the audiobook on the plane. For some reason, the book said, Japanese people had resisted learning English far more than other Asian countries.

"Good thing we've got an expert translator."

They both looked at Shane.

The man simply shrugged then nodded at the carousel. "This yours, Tara?"

It was. Soon, Shane and Craig had collected their luggage, and they were outside, waiting for the minibus to their hotel. The heat and humidity hit Craig hard. He'd read about the climate but had not been prepared for this. Just standing in the shade for a few minutes left him drenched with sweat. He could feel the energy being sapped away by the cloying moisture.

"See anything spooky?" Tara mopped her face with a tissue.

"Not so far," he replied.

Craig had braced himself for ghosts in the airport but had not seen any. Looking around, he saw foreigners and Japanese people in roughly equal proportions, all looking very much alive. Airports didn't seem to be haunted much, if at all, if his experience was any guide. He mentioned this to the others.

"Yeah," Tara agreed. "Most people die at home or in the hospital, not sitting in airport lounges. If people get sick here, they whisk them away pretty quickly."

Craig felt a sense of exhilaration despite the heat. He was in Japan. A guy who'd never amounted to much was suddenly thousands of miles from the U.S. and waiting to go to a luxury hotel in downtown Tokyo. Stark had pushed out the boat when it came to accommodation. It reflected the importance of the mission. Despite his dislike for Stark, Craig couldn't help but be impressed.

The bus to the midtown district arrived, and they piled on, with Craig taking a window seat to scout for ghosts. As they left Narita behind, he peered out at his first sight of Japan, but again drew a blank. After a while, he relaxed and tried to enjoy the view, which consisted mostly of hotels and parking lots. At least the bus was air-conditioned. Although that meant he was sitting in a puddle of rapidly cooling sweat.

"Still no ghosts," he told Tara, who was sitting next to him. "No obvious ones, at least."

Shane, in the seat behind, grunted his agreement.

"Maybe they're shy," Craig went on. "Self-effacing in death as in life."

"Over forty million people," Tara mused. "That's the greater Tokyo region. So how many ghosts are wandering if that's the live population?"

Craig had never thought about the ratio of the living to the dead. Back home, he had seen maybe one ghost per hundred or so living people. Tara had gone into more detail, arguing that roughly one in a thousand souls failed to immediately move on. However, over time, many would leave the earthly plane for one reason or another. She had come up with an attrition rate based on a typical ghost moving on after two years.

"I reckon the ghost population should be around a million in Tokyo if you include the metropolis. Now, if we assume only one in a thousand of those ghosts is potentially hostile, we're still looking at quite an onslaught…"

Craig felt disoriented. The thought of confronting even a fraction of that number was appalling. He had faced a handful of enemies in Grendon Mill, living and dead. Likewise in Scotland. He had come close to being killed in both places. Seeing his expression, Tara realized she was bringing him down.

"But that's my point. We've no reason to believe we'll be targeted. Chances are nobody knows we're even here. On the face of it, we're just another group of American tourists fixated on sightseeing and sushi."

Shane spoke up.

"Word through the grapevine is that the Sanagi cult uses ghosts and other supernatural beings. We should stay alert. Use the normal defenses. And get ourselves weapons ASAP."

One of Stark's contacts in Japan was supposed to supply the team with daggers and tasers, but not firearms. Japanese gun laws were as tough as those in the UK. In theory, a gun license could be obtained, but in practice, the screening process was too severe for most citizens, let alone a bunch of foreigners. Stark had made it clear that they were not to obtain illegal firearms, and for once, Craig agreed with the man.

The meeting with Stark's guy was tomorrow morning. In the meantime, they had around eighteen hours to kill. Craig, who felt jet lag looming, would have liked to spend that time sleeping. But, after they checked into their hotel, Tara insisted they go out for a meal.

"I'm famished, and we need to get acclimatized," she argued. "And you didn't eat anything on the plane."

Shane seconded the motion, and Craig realized he was hungry. Maybe a good meal would help. After freshening up, they met in the hotel lobby and set off into the bustling streets. It was around six thirty, and Tokyo's extended rush hour was still underway.

The first couple of restaurants they tried were full, as it was still tourist season. Then, Shane pointed to a modest-looking establishment down a side street.

"Traditional grub," he said.

"How traditional?" Craig asked. "I mean, it's not gonna be the fish that kill people, right?"

This prompted laughter before Tara assured him that the mortality rate for Japanese cuisine was below average. The restaurant was half-empty and, once Shane had spoken to the manager in fluent Japanese, they were shown to a corner table. Craig was glad to sit, as the heat was getting to him. A large fan spinning lazily in the center of the ceiling did little to alleviate the problem.

The menu was entirely in Japanese, accompanied by small photos of the various dishes. Craig had to rely on Shane to describe the ingredients.

"Squid ink?" Craig asked at one point. "Why?"

"Why not?" Shane retorted. "It's no weirder than eating clams or whatever. Just decide what you want before we all faint in this heat."

"I vote for that... spaghetti. Can't go wrong with spaghetti," said Craig, tapping the menu. He was too tired to think. "Just get me something to drink. But not booze."

Shane called over the waiter and gave their orders. Drinks arrived, and Craig gulped down a fruit tea. Slightly revived, he took time to study the restaurant's cozy interior. The Japanese customers nearby stole glances at the foreigners but didn't look directly at them. This tendency to avoid eye contact was mentioned in Craig's guidebook. However, as he peered into the gloom at the back, someone did meet his gaze. A young woman dressed in dark red, her hair elaborately coiffed, and her face pale in the semi-darkness. A dark mask covered the lower part of her face.

Craig leaned closer to Tara.

"Can you see her?" he whispered. "Just beside the serving hatch. Red kimono."

Tara peered and then shrugged.

"Nope. Not a living soul there."

The ghost continued to stare at Craig. He began to feel uncomfortable and looked away. The food arrived, and it looked and smelled appetizing. While the others opted for chopsticks, Craig settled for a fork. The spaghetti dish, called *mentaiko*, was tasty if unusual in flavor. Soon, he was wolfing it down. Now and then, he glanced up to see the woman in red still staring at him.

"Just ignore her; she's probably just a local haunter," Shane said. "How's the cod roe?"

Craig paused with his fork halfway to his mouth.

"What?"

"Fish eggs," Shane explained. "*Mentaiko* is spaghetti with cod roe, chili, and a few other things. Full of protein, fish eggs."

Craig put his laden fork down on his nearly empty plate.

"Next time," he said, "let's do KFC. My treat."

CHAPTER 14
ENCOUNTERS

Craig felt pressure in his bladder.

"I gotta take a leak. Will that be a problem?"

Tara pointed at the restroom. The door was a few feet from the ghost, who was still motionless and staring. Craig got up and, smiling awkwardly at the waiter, sidled past a party of suited business types who were drinking beer. He was determined not to attract attention. If the ghost did anything short of a direct attack, he would ignore her.

The woman in red kept staring as he passed her. She was taller than most Japanese women and seemed to be holding something concealed by her crossed hands. Craig got the impression that she was smiling behind the mask. He relaxed once he was inside the restroom.

He was washing his hands when a pale, masked face appeared in the mirror.

"Okay." He held up his hands. "Ghosts can't kill me, lady. So maybe just not try, right?"

The woman in red spoke, her words slightly muffled by the mask.

"Watashi, kirei?"

Craig had no idea what she was saying, but it was a question, which implied a correct answer. One that he was unable to give.

"I'm sorry, I can't help you," he said and then remembered the Japanese for "sorry". "*Sumisamen. Sumisamen.* I don't understand."

She uncrossed her hands to reveal a large pair of scissors that gleamed wickedly in the bathroom's harsh light. Craig felt suddenly less sure of himself. Maybe different rules applied to ghosts here.

The woman moved forward, passing out of the mirror and through the sinks. Then, the woman lowered her mask, and Craig gasped. The woman's mouth ended in angry red slits that extended back to her ears.

A slit-mouthed woman…

Then, he recalled the audiobook's list of *yokai*. The slit-mouthed woman was not, technically, a ghost. Perhaps she could stab him. He retreated until he was inside a stall. He remembered Tara's iron brooch. He wished he'd had the sense to ask her to loan it to him.

The restroom door opened, and Craig saw Shane reflected in the mirror beyond the ghost. The spirit turned to face Shane and repeated her question, who shot back something in Japanese. It was brief, perhaps a single word.

She spoke again, a different question it seemed, raising the scissors, and advancing on Shane. He stood his ground and snapped out a reply, a different word or phrase than last time. The ghost stopped, and her shoulders slumped. Then she faded slowly, losing definition. The last thing to vanish was the grotesque, malformed smile.

"Jeez," Craig said. "So that was our first *yokai*?"

Shane looked a little disdainful.

"Kuchisake-Onna, right. You should do more research, my man! First time she asks, 'Am I beautiful?' You say, 'Yes.' Then, she takes off the mask and asks, 'How about now?' If you give the right answer, she has to vamoose and reconsider. Wrong answer, she attacks you."

Craig thought about that.

"But what's the right answer?"

Shane grinned.

"You tell her she looks okay. You know, average. Passable but nothing special. No woman can stand that, living or dead. Come on out if you're done. I need a drink."

"That was no accidental encounter," Tara said when they told her what had happened. "We used our names, so it wouldn't be hard for the

Sanagi cult to track us down. They sent one of their country's heavy hitters. She's a true urban legend."

Craig thought back to his first sight of the entity. Had she followed them or been waiting? He tried to remember if the figure in the blood-red kimono had been waiting in the shadows when they'd been seated, but he was not sure.

Tara began Googling the slit-mouthed woman while Shane ordered beer for himself and Craig.

"Interesting," Tara commented. "The story of Kuchisake-Onna is a bit like the Chelsea Smilers in London. But the Japanese version is older and more detailed. Wow, in the seventies, people got so scared of her, that parents started walking their kids to school. In a country with a low crime rate like Japan, that's major-league fear. But she's not been reported much lately."

"Guess it was a special occasion," Shane remarked sourly.

"What I want to know," Craig kept his voice steady, "is whether she could have killed me. Is she more dangerous than a regular ghost? Are the rules different here?"

Tara frowned, scrolling.

"Maybe. Different cultures have a different paranormal vibe, I dare say. I've thought about that a lot. The way ordinary people think, stuff they believe, might create a kind of… call it an energy field. It would explain why European vampires are different than the undead in other countries. Same with shapeshifters. You find them in all cultures, but they have different natures, each with a unique MO. Just so happens that *yokai* are unique to Japan. They seem to overlap with ghosts and demons to some extent. And there are a lot of them."

There was a lull in conversation as the waitress arrived with two glasses of Sapporo beer. Shane thanked her as she set the drinks down. She smiled and said a few words. Craig watched the brief conversation, still a little astounded by Shane's linguistic ability. To master any language with unnatural speed was a talent worth having. An ordinary guy could have gotten very rich by those means alone. But, of course, you couldn't call Shane Ryan ordinary.

"You don't have to stop talking about weird stuff just because there's a local nearby." Shane took a gulp of beer. "Most people only speak a few dozen words of English if that. Anyone who has good English and overhears us would just think we're talking about a game or a TV show or whatever."

"Okay." Tara set her phone down. "It seems like our lady in the mask is borderline. A ghostly *yokai*, maybe. Or a turbocharged ghost. The story goes that she was the wife of a samurai who was always away from home. She took lovers, he found out, and he mutilated her face. She took this badly and committed suicide, then started attacking people with scissors. If you answer her question incorrectly—saying she doesn't look so hot— she makes your face like hers. Or she slices you into little pieces, opinions vary."

"You think she'll be back?" Craig asked.

"Probably," Shane said. "I doubt if calling her average-looking is going to work more than once."

"Nah," Tara confirmed. "It confuses her for a bit. But she can be very persistent."

A thought struck Craig.

"Is there anything about her in that book of prophecy?" he asked Tara.

"Good point!" She took out the slim, dog-eared volume. The two men sipped their beer as she scrutinized the tiny print. While the book had fewer than a hundred pages, it packed a lot in. Thaddeus Crutchley had been a garrulous prophet.

"Nothing about women with slitty mouths," she said, "but there is something else. Kind of spooky."

She picked up the book and sat back in her seat as the others listened attentively.

"'The seeker will voyage to the land of the Golden Flower King. There, he will be guided by a knight of the most sorrowful countenance. This knight shall wield both a greater sword and a lesser sword, as is the custom of that country.'"

"Two swords of different sizes. That must be a samurai," Shane mused. "But the stuff about the golden flower makes no sense to me."

Tara smiled at Craig.

"And you?"

He admitted he hadn't even gotten the samurai part.

"Okay," Tara sighed. "You boys didn't do enough background reading. The Chrysanthemum Throne was a common English term for the Japanese monarchy. And the flower we know, which came to the West from China by the way, gets its name from the Greek. *Chrysanthemon*. It means 'golden flower'. So, the land of the Golden Flower King is where we are right now."

"That Crutchley guy should have taken his act on the road," Shane grunted.

Craig twisted around and looked out into the street, half-expecting a samurai to appear. All he saw was the quiet throng of Tokyoites.

"If Crutchley is right, we have someone to meet up with," Shane said, "but I'll bet your prophet hasn't given us a map reference?"

Tara riffled through the yellowed pages, running a finger down lines of faded print. Eventually, she shook her head.

"No, it's mostly gobbledygook about the end of the world and how bad it'll be for sinners, which seems to include just about everybody. Usual prophetic language. A lot of bets being hedged."

They decided against dessert and headed back to the hotel instead. Craig spotted a few ghosts along the way. At first, he thought they might be living people zoned out on street corners or in doorways. But the bustling crowds soon caused people to walk through the phantoms. Now and then, Craig saw a pedestrian hesitate, looking puzzled, and then move on. The ghosts involved in these collisions didn't seem affected by them. Unlike the ghosts he was used to, those in Tokyo were oddly inert. They just stood there, staring blankly.

"Yeah," Tara said when he pointed this out, "I guess that's because they still want to be part of living society, but they're excluded from it. This is a highly collectivist culture. The pressure to conform is massive. Everyone likes to feel part of a group, and individualism—as we think of it—is kind of frowned upon. To become a ghost means being cut off from family, colleagues, and friends."

"Death is a shock to the system," Shane concurred. "I guess some of 'em never get over it."

They saw dozens more motionless ghosts. They eventually encountered two more active specters, though. The first was a ghost girl. She seemed very young and reminded Craig of Chloe, as she had the same vibe. She was wandering through the crowd and trying in vain to attract the attention of men. Shane speculated that she had died unmarried and was still searching for a husband.

"That is very sexist," Tara remarked, "but also probably true in this context."

When the girl noticed that they could see her, she looked alarmed and retreated, vanishing into the wall of a 7-Eleven.

"Not into white guys, I guess," Shane observed.

More striking was the phantom samurai standing on a corner near the famous Shibuya crossing. He was clad in a blue and white kimono rather than armor, but two swords sheathed at his waist proclaimed his status. As hundreds of office workers and tourists hurried across the busy intersection, the warrior stood coolly on the sidewalk, regarding the mass of humanity with a sad, thoughtful expression. Every so often, he stepped deftly aside to avoid the touch of the living.

"Could be our guy." Craig described the ghost to Tara.

"He's supposed to guide us," she said excitedly. "Does he look friendly?"

The Americans approached the ghost cautiously. The dead samurai saw them coming but did not react.

"Well?" Tara asked. "Is he the two-swords knight or what?"

Craig admitted that the samurai did not look particularly helpful.

"How are we supposed to know if he's the right one?" he wondered aloud. "There must be a lot of them around. That said, his countenance is kind of sorrowful."

"What should I ask?" Shane said as they got within earshot.

"Maybe ask about Sanagi," Craig suggested.

The ghost's eyes widened at the mention of the cult leader. He raised one hand and made a finger-flicking gesture that Craig interpreted as "go away". He stopped dead.

"No," Shane said, "I think that means 'come here'. At least we've got his attention."

Craig stepped forward hesitantly until he calculated he was just over a sword's length away. Shane, by his side, fired off some questions. Craig heard the name "Sanagi" several times. The warrior looked puzzled and replied with a lot of rapid-fire Japanese. After a couple of minutes, Shane turned to Craig.

"His name is Shiro, and he died about a hundred and fifty years ago, but not in battle. That's one of the reasons he's still hanging around. He didn't die a warrior's death, but he's kind of cagey about how he passed on. Anyhow, he says Sanagi is not dead, and yet, he has died many times."

"Does that mean Sanagi has been reincarnated?" Tara asked. "Because that's Buddhism, not Shintoism. Is Sanagi doing mix-and-match religions?"

Shane shrugged.

"To be honest, what this guy is saying sounds more like poetry than information. He's the definition of old school. He probably whiles away the years writing haikus in his head."

The samurai looked closely at Craig, who felt uncomfortable. The ghost then switched his gaze to Tara, and then back to Shane. The forbidding expression softened slightly, and the ghost spoke a few words before closing his eyes.

"What's going on?" Tara asked.

"He said something to Shane," Craig explained. "Now he looks like he's meditating."

The two waited. Shane shrugged.

"He said we will find what we seek, and then our stories will end. Which sounds kind of ominous."

CHAPTER 15

THE WARRIOR'S GATE

The samurai spirit opened his eyes again and gave Craig a piercing look. Then he rapped out a few words to Shane, turned, and strode off through the crowd.

"I guess we follow him," Shane said. "He said he'll take us to a forgotten gateway that leads to wisdom. More poetic stuff."

"Can we trust him?" Tara asked.

"I think so. I'm getting an okay vibe from the guy," Shane said, and set off after the figure in blue and white.

"Military types," Tara remarked and followed.

Shiro moved swiftly, deftly stepping around the living where possible. Sometimes, it wasn't. Craig saw the ghost walk through a line of chattering schoolgirls in sailor-suit uniforms. Eyes widened and conversation faltered for a minute. Then, the talk resumed, and the girls passed. The same thing happened with a coffee vendor, and a businessman staring at his phone. Every person who brushed past Shiro hesitated, looked up, and then shrugged off the incident. Craig had seen the same thing many times back home. It was easy to discount the inexplicable shudder and hint of strangeness in everyday life.

We are such intensely visual creatures, he thought. *If it can't be seen, it can usually be ignored.*

"What did he mean by a gateway?" Craig asked as he drew alongside Shane.

"He used the word *torii*, which is a gate to a Shinto shrine," Shane explained. "So maybe that's where we're going. A shrine significant to

Shiro in some way, I guess."

Craig looked around them. This was downtown Tokyo, not the outskirts or a quiet suburb. Night was drawing in, and neon signs were beginning to outshine the overcast sky. Immense office buildings and malls vied for space with restaurants, coffee shops, boutiques, and quirkier businesses. He saw a store dedicated to plush toys with anime themes, and another that specialized in old-style cameras and stereos. There were lots of vending machines, with small clusters of people buying drinks and snacks.

There were also hints of the sleazy underbelly that every big city has. Craig peered down one garishly lit street to see rows of girls in skimpy maid outfits handing out flyers. Most of the passersby treated them as if they were invisible. Tara explained that they were promoting themed cafes and bars where various unusual services were offered.

"Maid cafes are popular. They sometimes combine it with a cat theme. See the girl with the ears? Oh, and she's got a cute tail, too."

Craig only just stopped himself from making a "piece of tail" joke. The cat-maid girl saw him looking and smiled, waving a flyer. He looked away in confusion. Tara laughed.

"They even meow at you. Some guys seem to like it."

"Hard to imagine a temple in a neighborhood like this," Craig remarked.

"Japan: Land of Contrasts," Tara said in a ponderous mockumentary voice. "Seriously, you'd be surprised how much of the old culture survives."

As if on cue, the crowds thinned out and the buildings grew less flashy and imposing. Shiro turned off the main thoroughfare and into one of the ubiquitous alleyways. Craig noticed for the first time how much narrower Tokyo was, given the vastness of the city. In the U.S., everything was built with cars in mind. Here, not so much.

A couple of young men smoking cigarettes watched as they passed.

They gave no sign of seeing the long-dead warrior who led the small party. Craig wondered how many Japanese people could see ghosts or at least sense them. A higher percentage than in the West? And did such a deeply conformist society make it harder or easier for ghost seers to get by? A quotation from his book on Japan came to mind. "The nail that stands out gets hammered down." He guessed most seers would keep quiet about it.

A light rain began to fall, growing steadily heavier. It didn't seem to mitigate the heat and humidity. Craig felt sure that he was squelching in places nobody should squelch. The sun had set. The alley was dimly lit, but Craig could still make out Shiro striding ahead of them. Given the limitations of a ghost's movement—a radius of about a mile from his haunted object—he wondered if the shrine was Shiro's base. Ghosts were almost always linked to a specific object. In Shiro's case, it might be something obvious like a sword, or a trivial item like a rice bowl. Whatever it was, it had survived centuries in the heart of this metropolis. That implied something well hidden.

"There it is," Tara said.

Craig could just make out the *torii*, its distinctive shape framed against the glow of yellow lanterns. He had a flashback to math class. The gate was shaped something like the Greek letter *Pi* but with an extra bar across the top. As they got closer, he saw that the *torii* was painted red. Beyond it was a modest structure approached up a short flight of steps. He tried to remember the snippets he'd learned about Shinto. The shrines were believed to be the homes of Japan's ancient gods, the *kami*. Offerings of money meant that some shrines were prosperous and looked it. But it seemed that the deity here was modest, if not downright shabby. There was no sign of life. Shiro walked up to the gate and stopped just short of the elegant wooden portal. He bowed, then walked through.

"We do what he does," Shane said. "As in, we keep to the left side of the path. Only the god walks down the middle."

The three followed the ghost through the *torii*. Perhaps it was Craig's imagination, but he felt that the shadows deepened as he crossed the threshold. He had the sudden sense of being watched but could not see anyone, living or dead. However, he was happy that the rain had suddenly eased off, with just a few stray droplets pattering onto the flagstones.

Shiro approached a small wooden trough into which water flowed from a pipe. A metal dipper hung from a post. The ghost disappeared as he touched the dipper, then reappeared after a second. This repeated several times until he was done.

Another ritual to follow—cleansing with pure, flowing water. This was something Craig recalled from his book. Wash each hand, then your mouth, but do not put your mouth to the dipper. Instead, you poured water into the palm of your hand and then raised it to your mouth.

"That's odd." Tara took the dipper from Shane. "These things are usually made of wood, not iron."

"Is it significant?" Craig asked.

"Might be, given iron's effect on ghosts and demons."

They walked up a flight of stone steps to the shrine proper. Still, no living human appeared, and Craig got the odd impression that they were no longer in the heart of the metropolis. Tokyo's omnipresent neon glow had faded so that only moonlight filtered through low clouds. Buildings still loomed around them, but they were unlit, vague shapes. The roar of the city traffic had diminished to a distant murmur.

"Anyone else think it's getting weird?" he asked.

"I think we crossed some kind of paranormal threshold," Tara said quietly. "I guess it took us somewhere else. A quieter place."

The temple was illuminated by two yellow lanterns decorated with Japanese characters. Shiro pulled at a rope, and a bell sounded. Then, he bowed twice, clapped twice, and then bowed again. This was, Shane explained quietly, to attract the attention of the *kami*. Craig found the idea amusing. As if a god needed to be roused like a dozing nightwatchman. But then, he wondered what an immortal being would do with its time.

After a while, a *kami* might well become indifferent to the antics of humans. Our lives, so very brief, would blur into background noise. In a way, it was surprising that a mere clap could stir an immortal out of some unimaginable reverie.

"We need to make an offering," Shane explained. "After you do the bell-and-clapping thing, throw it into the box inside the doorway. A five-yen coin is standard. Nothing smaller. And when you're done, move over to the side. But never turn your back on the shrine. That's a mark of disrespect."

Tara went first, ringing the bell vigorously and then tossing her coin. It clattered on wood. There was no hint of contact with metal. It seemed no offerings had been made here lately. Or maybe, Craig wondered, the priest here was very quick to scoop up the dough? That seemed unlikely. Shane followed Tara, ringing the bell vigorously, his two claps echoing like gunshots. After Shane made his offering, Craig stepped up.

He heard someone snicker. Tara, perhaps? It had a high, feminine tone, but she would never be so frivolous. Ignoring the sound, he bowed, clapped, and bowed once more. Then, he groped in his pocket for the right coin. He was just throwing his five yen when the snickering sounded again, followed by a voice. It was high-pitched and sneering. Far more disturbing, though, was the fact that it spoke in English.

"Sanagi welcomes you!"

Craig spun around and gazed into the shadows. Too late, he recalled that he should not turn his back on the *kami*. Shane swore. Something stirred behind Craig, and he sensed movement in the darkness within the shrine. But when he looked back, he saw nothing in the faint lamplight.

"Where's Shiro?" Shane asked.

The samurai was nowhere to be seen, but something else was appearing. The right-hand lantern over the doorway of the shrine was swinging from side to side, its light flickering uncertainly. Tara stood directly underneath it. Craig pointed and shouted a warning. Tara looked up. At the same moment, a face appeared in the lantern.

Yokai, Craig thought. *Not necessarily dangerous, but better safe than sorry.*

The face grimaced at Craig and then looked at Tara. She fell into a crouching run, but the lantern detached itself from its hook and dropped. As it fell, the entity transformed into a grotesque, oversized human head. Long black hair framed a pale face with tiny, malevolent eyes. A huge mouth gaped.

At first, Craig thought Tara would dodge easily, but the entity changed direction, no longer plummeting but flying in pursuit. A dark tongue unrolled out of the vast mouth, impossibly long and thick. It lashed out at Tara, the blow striking her on the side of the head. In the light of the remaining lantern, Craig saw her eyes roll back and her facial muscles grow slack. She fell heavily onto the wooden decking. Then, the *yokai* swooped toward Craig.

CHAPTER 16
HEADS, YOU LOSE

Instead of dodging backward, Craig tried to roll forward. He felt the head thing swoop over him, its hair trailing. Tara had fallen onto her side, unconscious. Craig grabbed her jacket and tore off her iron brooch, flinging himself sideways just in time. The *yokai* swooped again, more slowly this time. The bloated, piggy-eyed visage hovered a couple of feet away, right over Tara.

"Surrender to us, Craig Ellison," it said, "or I will slay this one."

Craig hurled the sharp-edged brooch. The *yokai* was surprised, and its little eyes widened as the iron penetrated and stuck to its right cheek. The mouth opened wide in a roar of rage, but it did not disappear.

"You will suffer!" the *yokai* screeched.

The wound in its cheek was turning black, and veins of darkness radiated out. Craig picked up the brooch.

"Bet you wish you had hands now, huh," he said.

The head thing bellowed and hurtled toward him. Craig lashed out, but the *yokai* slowed and veered to one side at the last moment. Its tongue flicked out and wrapped around Craig's wrist. Instantly, a pain like a wasp sting but a hundred times worse gripped his arm. He felt faint and nauseous.

Tara.

He couldn't fail her, but the darkness was already growing deeper. Nobody could stand such agony. The ugly, marred face of the *yokai* looked down at him. He couldn't let it win, couldn't let that hideous visage be the last thing he saw. He waited for the creature to get nearer before delivering as strong a kick as he could. The toe of his sneaker connected with Tara's brooch, driving it deeper. A black fluid spurted from the wound, thick and stinking.

The *yokai*'s scream heralded a diminution in Craig's pain. It uncoiled its tongue and flew upward out of reach. He managed to stand as the monster circled him as he turned, waiting for it to attack. Then, he saw a blur of movement in the lamplight. The *yokai* sensed the new threat a moment too late. Shane brought the dipper down onto the *yokai* with immense force, smashing it out of the air so that it bounced on the wooden boards.

Iron, Craig thought. *An iron weapon right there in plain sight.*

Shane brought the dipper down onto the *yokai* again and again, pummeling it until it collapsed into a puddle of grayish slime. All the features were gone. Only the mass of black hair remained, shifting slightly as the remains bubbled and smoked. Then, it seeped into the wooden boards that fronted the shrine, leaving nothing but a smear of grease and Tara's brooch. Craig bent and picked up the brooch, wiping off the gunk on his pants.

"Did I miss something?"

Tara was trying to raise herself on one elbow. After a few moments, it became clear that she was concussed, or something like it. The shock of the *yokai*'s tongue impacting her head had been far more severe than Craig's injury. His arm was still numb from the sting, but the pain was dwindling, though not as fast as he would like.

"Let's get out of here," Shane said.

The men lifted Tara and helped her down the steps and toward the gate.

"You think Shiro led us into a trap?" Craig asked.

"Looks like it," Shane admitted. "But I got an okay vibe from the guy, and I'm not usually—hey, speak of the devil."

Craig followed Shane's gaze and saw a figure in blue and white

THE ISLAND OF SHADOWS

standing outside the *torii*. It was Shiro, standing with his arms crossed over his chest. They paused by the water trough, waiting for the ghost to speak, but Shiro remained impassive with his head bowed and his eyes downcast.

"Guess we have to go through him," Shane said. "Here. I don't need any weapons to take a ghost."

He handed the iron dipper to Craig and walked toward the phantom samurai.

"My brooch," Tara said weakly. "I can maybe…"

Craig held it in front of her. It wobbled in his hand, shot diagonally upward, and then spun down to the flagstones.

"Guess not," Tara sighed.

Craig propped her against the water trough and ran to catch up with Shane. Shiro had raised his head and was looking at the Americans, but the ghost had not uncrossed his arms. Craig noted that he stood just outside the *torii*, not under the wooden beams.

"You led us into a trap," Shane said in coldly.

Craig looked at his friend in surprise. How could Shiro understand the accusation? But then came another surprise. The samurai replied in English, accented but grammatically perfect.

"It is a necessary ordeal. As a warrior, you must understand that sometimes even an ally might act like an enemy, and vice versa. And it is not yet complete."

As Shiro spoke, Craig had the weird sensation that the ghost's mouth was moving oddly. The syllables he heard did not match the ones Shiro's lips were forming. Then, he grasped the situation. Shiro was not speaking English, but Japanese, and Craig could still understand him.

"Whatever," Shane snapped. "You gonna stand aside?"

The ghost finally moved, opening his arms in a gesture that might have been one of welcome. Shiro moved back into the gloom beyond the gate.

"Okay, come on," Shane said.

Craig walked Tara through the *torii* and stopped. Shane, too, had halted.

Shiro had vanished, but that was not what startled them.

"Hey…" Tara said blearily. "We got turned around."

Ahead of the trio stood the Shinto shrine, complete with steps, a water trough, and two yellow lanterns about the doorway. Craig half-expected the lanterns to shapeshift, but they only hung there, casting a soft radiance over the impossible scene.

"Back," Shane said.

Craig turned and guided Tara under the double crossbars of the gate, only to find himself in the same place.

"Dirty little trick with dimensions," Shane remarked, "unless it's an illusion."

It felt real to Craig. They tried again, with the same result. Then, Craig felt Tara growing unsteady, and guided her to the steps so she could sit.

"What's happening?" she asked.

"I think it's kind of an escape room situation," Craig suggested. "Shiro said the ordeal wasn't over."

Shane shot him a sharp look.

"You understood him?"

"Yeah, but I don't know why. I could just suddenly understand Japanese."

Tara looked from one man to the other.

"I thought he was speaking English. What the hell? Why would we acquire Shane's special ability?"

Craig had an inkling, but before he could find words, he noticed movement at the top of the stairs. They were not alone. He felt a chill and had the sudden thought that it might be the slit-mouth ghost, coming for revenge. The figure began to carefully descend the steps. Craig took out his phone and turned on the flashlight. The blue-white glow revealed a normal-looking Japanese woman in a green kimono. She had long black hair that flowed over her shoulders.

"Hello!" she said with a friendly smile. "Are you lost? You look lost. And very far from home! Such strange faces. I confess that I am intrigued."

"Who are you?" Shane demanded.

"I am merely a wanderer like yourselves."

"What is your name?" Craig asked.

The doll-like face was marred briefly by a frown.

"I am ashamed to say that I have forgotten. Perhaps I will remember soon. Is it important?"

"Are you a ghost?" Craig asked.

The green-clad woman reached the foot of the steps and stopped, peering up at Craig. She was tiny, shorter than five feet tall. She was also extremely pretty in a delicate way, with a tiny rosebud mouth and large eyes.

"I am not a ghost, or so I believe," she said. "Please, let us not be too formal."

The green-clad woman extended a tiny, delicate hand. Craig reached out.

"Careful," Shane hissed.

Ready to leap back, Craig took the woman's fingers in his. They were cool but had none of the piercing chill that came from touching a ghost. He quickly pulled his hand away.

"Not a ghost," he told the others, "but maybe something else."

The woman raised her hand to her mouth and emitted a girlish giggle.

"I am sorry," she said, "but you men are so big and strong, and I am so small and weak. But you fear me."

"Can you show us the way out of here?" Craig asked. "We would be very grateful."

The woman tilted her head.

"I can lead you to safety. I am hungry."

It was an odd way to put it.

"Okay," Craig said. "If you show us the way out, we'll buy you dinner. Deal?"

He heard Tara groan slightly. He grasped the problem a second later. Making deals with strange entities was seldom a smart idea.

"You promise you will feed me?" the woman asked.

Craig looked at Tara, who shrugged, and then at Shane.

"Hell yeah," Shane declared loudly. "It's a deal."

CHAPTER 17
THE HUNGER

The woman smiled, walked forward a few paces, and then stopped.

"If you will walk ahead of me? To the gateway?"

Tara struggled to her feet. Craig noted that the kimono hobbled the woman's movement so she couldn't run. This did not reassure him much. He was halfway expecting her to transform into something even more monstrous than their earlier antagonists. He clutched the iron dipper tightly in his right hand while supporting Tara with his left.

"She wants us to turn our backs on her," Shane said quietly. "Don't fall for it."

"By all means, walk backward," the woman said immediately.

"Why don't you walk ahead of us?" Tara demanded. "That's how you show someone the way, isn't it?"

The woman's serene smile did not falter. She continued to look at Craig as she spoke again.

"Very well," she said, "but please extinguish your light. It might attract unwanted attention."

That seemed reasonable. Craig turned off the flashlight on his phone and stepped aside, gesturing at the *torii*. Taking tiny precise steps, the woman walked past and headed for the entrance. In the mellow light of the shrine lanterns, she looked ethereal, otherworldly. She probably was.

As the woman passed Craig, he saw that her hair was even longer than he'd thought. The great, dark mane stretched down her back and almost trailed on the ground. It rippled slightly as she walked, catching the light of the lanterns. Something like a barrette was across the back of her head, but it was hard to make out in the dim light.

"Any idea?" he whispered to Tara.

"Nope," she replied. "This one doesn't ring a bell. But there are so many *yokai*. And some are benevolent."

They followed the petite figure to the gate, where she paused under the red-lacquered beams. Without turning around, she spoke again.

"You promise to feed me? I am very hungry."

"We promise," Craig said impatiently.

The woman stepped over the threshold, taking a dozen or so tiny paces. The three followed. Craig felt something stirring in the darkness. Glancing back, he saw what might have been a shadow flit under one of the lanterns. Then, he felt Tara stiffen and gasp against his side. He looked ahead to see that the same trick had been played. They were facing the shrine once more.

Shane stormed. "Listen, lady—"

"Now you must feed me," the sweet, high voice said.

The green-clad figure still had its back to them, but something hard to make out was happening to the thing on the back of the woman's head. Craig lifted his phone and flicked on the flashlight. A huge, gaping mouth had opened amid the mass of hair, a red maw lined with inhumanly large teeth.

"Oh, my God!" Tara whispered.

"Okay, no need to panic," Shane said, "but maybe we'd better—"

The huge mane of hair reared up like a cobra and struck at him. Black strands wove around Shane's neck, arms, and legs. Despite her small size, the woman possessed preternatural strength. Shane was flung onto his back in seconds, and then the hair dragged him toward the entity. Still with her back to her prey, the woman knelt to bring the huge mouth closer to Shane.

Craig let go of Tara and ran forward, swinging the iron dipper. But the woman thing was more than ready for him. A thick rope of hair detached itself from Shane's body and swatted the improvised weapon from Craig's hand. It clattered on the flagstones as more hair encircled Craig and pinned him down.

The creature's voice was louder now.

"I. Am. HUNGRY!"

Craig, struggling vainly against the black strands, saw Tara crawling toward the dipper on her hands and knees. She was having trouble exerting her power at a distance and needed to get closer to lift it with her mind. But their monstrous assailant was too quick. Hair encircled Tara's left ankle and jerked viciously, so she fell heavily with a plaintive yelp.

Shane had been dragged to within a foot of the mouth. Struggling and cursing, he held steady in place for a few seconds. Then the creature yanked him closer, and the huge jaws snapped at his face. Shane avoided the bite somehow and pulled away, but his Herculean efforts could only last so long.

"Tara, the dipper," Craig shouted.

The iron handle was lying just out of reach. Tara lay motionless, either unconscious or too stunned to react. Craig's rage and frustration overcame his panic as the idea that had formed earlier returned. It was a paranormal Hail Mary, but he had to try. He focused his mind on the dipper and imagined lifting it as if he had a third arm that could stretch an absurd distance. The dipper rocked slightly, then rose.

He'd been right. They had shared Shane's power after passing through the gate once. Now, they shared Tara's. He sent the dipper skimming at a low level into the side of the creature's head. It was not especially fast or accurate, but it did the trick. After a satisfying clang, the woman thing reeled, and Craig felt its grip relax.

"Shane, we can TK like Tara," he cried, picking up the dipper.

The monster had recovered enough to focus on Craig and sent more writhing ropes of hair to stifle him, but he didn't need to move to strike back. He flung the iron implement at the entity again, this time striking it in its hideous second mouth. The thing seemed to grasp the situation, however, and Craig felt cool, rough strands circling his throat as it began to choke the life out of him. He gasped, unable to avoid panic, and his grip on the weapon failed.

The gloom around him grew deeper, and the yellow lamplight faded. Craig knew he was dying with an almost reassuring certainty. A pounding in his ears rose to an all-embracing crescendo as the darkness flooded his mind and soul.

Then he heard a fierce, resounding clang of metal. Then another, and then a series of metallic impacts like someone was hammering. The world returned to Craig's vision, and he felt the hair relaxing its grip. He sat up in time to see Shane standing over what looked like a great mound of hair. He had the dipper in his hand and was bringing it down on the black mass. The impact of metal on bone made Craig flinch. After a few more brutal blows, the clanging sound changed in timbre and became muffled. The hair mound collapsed. Shane struck the pavement of the shrine and cursed at the recoil. A moment later, the dark mane was gone.

"Smart thinking, and thanks," Shane said, walking over to Craig and offering his free hand.

Tara was sitting up and rubbing her ankle. They helped her upright. After a few moments, she was up to speed and thinking things over.

"So… if we go through the gate again, we get your power?" she said to Craig.

Craig shook his head.

"I think we have to go through as part of this ordeal. There has to be another threat to overcome."

They looked around. There was no hint of anything out of the ordinary. The only evidence of what had happened to them was a badly dented dipper with a bent handle. That, and the bruises. Craig wondered what paranormal threat would appear next. They were fatigued from the flight. He felt a pang of resentment toward his companions for not doing the obvious.

If we'd just stayed in the goddamn hotel...

"Look!"

Tara was pointing up at the temple. A human figure was silhouetted against the lantern on the right. It moved forward, and something about it seemed familiar.

"Shiro," Shane hissed.

As reached the top of the steps, Craig saw that it was indeed the ghostly samurai. With a swift movement, Shiro drew his long sword. He took up a defensive position as if to stop the Americans from reaching the shrine.

"You think that thing will stop me?" Shane shouted, climbing the stairs.

Tara spoke up.

"Let's try and take him out from a distance first, yeah?"

Shane hesitated and then nodded. It made sense.

"All together, then," he said, and held the battered dipper in the air.

Craig focused on the iron handle, imagining his invisible hand grasping it. He felt some resistance, a lack of control. Then, he realized that the three of them were working against each other to some extent.

"Let's just chuck it straight at him, Shane," he suggested. "Nothing fancy. And Tara, maybe guide it?"

The trio stood in a line, concentrating hard. It worked. The dipper flew upward diagonally, turning over in flight. A mangled iron implement, almost comical, but with the power to dispel a ghost on impact.

Craig expected Shiro to dodge, but the ghost did nothing of the sort. Instead, he took a quick step back, swung his curved sword, and sliced the dipper in half.

"Hey," Tara said. "That's cheating!"

CHAPTER 18
THE DEAD CAN'T DIE

"I'll take the bowl side," Shane said.

Craig grasped it at once. The two iron fragments rose into the air and swooped down toward Shiro from opposite sides. Again, the warrior was too fast for them. He smashed the bowl of the dipper away with the flat side of his sword and then slashed the handle into two smaller parts. The trio responded, after initially fumbling, by sending all three fragments toward their foe. But Shiro, still descending the stairs, effortlessly anticipated their attacks and sent the dipper bowl flying into the night, out of sight. The larger of the handle shards followed. The remaining piece of iron fell to the steps as Tara lost energy and maybe heart.

"The sword!" Craig cried. "It must be steel, right?"

"Right. All together!" Shane responded.

Three minds focused on the katana blade. Craig felt a response, an undeniable sense of slim, metallic hardness, but he could not grasp it. No matter how hard he tried, his newfound skill had no effect. While it was very much a material weapon, the sword was somehow immune to Tara's power.

"Just hit him," Tara gasped. "Pluck out his eyes. Stop his heart."

It was logical, in a ruthless way. If Shiro's sword had become solid, surely the ghost was now a living man? Craig lashed out with his dwindling psychokinetic energy. He tried to shove Shiro off-balance to slow him down, but the oily, frictionless feeling defeated him again. There was nothing to grasp and nothing to strike at.

The warrior was invulnerable.

Shiro reached the bottom of the steps and did not pause. He advanced, holding his sword ahead of him with both hands. Craig, supporting Tara, retreated behind Shane. He looked around in desperation for something that could be used as a weapon. But nothing was nearby except the wooden water trough and the *torii*.

"Run for it," Shane said. "Get her out. If this is the last test…"

Craig started to protest, then realized he would be wasting time. He turned and helped Tara through the gateway. He expected to be confronted with the shrine again, the trough, and the flight of steps. Instead, they stumbled into the alley they had come along to get here. The vast neon heart of Tokyo lit up the sky, and the sudden roar of city traffic was almost shocking.

"Hey!"

Craig turned as fast as he could without letting Tara go. Shane was facing off against Shiro, and it looked hopelessly one-sided. Shiro stomped forward a pace, lowering his sword to point the tip at Shane's face. The distance from blade to flesh was no more than six inches.

"Oh Jesus," Tara whispered. "Oh God, no."

Shiro raised his sword and swung it around in a vicious arc on Shane's left. Craig realized that the samurai intended to decapitate the Marine. The steel caught the lamplight. The effect might have been beautiful if it had not been a killing blow. Except that Shane did not die. An eyeblink later, he was standing impassively in front of his opponent. The next, he was rolling forward under the slashing blade, closing the distance with lightning speed.

Shane struck Shiro's legs and took the warrior down. There was a blur of movement, with Shiro's blue and white kimono flapping wildly as the two rolled across the flagstones. Then, Shane was standing above the samurai with his enemy's sword in his hand. The point of the katana was leveled at Shiro's throat.

"Bugger me sideways," Tara exclaimed.

Shiro, his face still devoid of emotion, spoke loudly and clearly.

"Finish me. Now I am humiliated. All is lost."

Shane waited a moment before lifting the blade. As he did so, the tip nicked the samurai's cheek, and a thin trickle of blood flowed black in the poor light. Then, as suddenly as it had appeared, the wound vanished.

"No," Shane said. "That's absurd, and you know it. You can't kill a dead man any more than you can knock up a pregnant woman. So, what's this really about?"

The samurai smiled, and for the first time, Craig saw the depths of the man's sadness.

"The wisdom of the warrior." Shiro rose gracefully to his feet. "You must pass through if we are to complete the ritual. Like a delicate flower in a mountain storm, its time is short."

Shane lowered the sword and then, to Craig's surprise, offered it to Shiro. The warrior took it, flicked it to one side, then sheathed it expertly. Then, Shiro gestured to Shane to precede him into the alley. Shane did so without hesitating. As the warrior passed under the red crossbeams, Craig saw a glimmer of mist surrounding the compact form. The color of the fine kimono seemed to fade a little. Shiro stopped just outside the bounds of the temple.

"Once more, I am a thing of mist and shadow." He stretched out his hand to Craig. "Pity this humble and contrite ghost who has lingered so many years. I ask you to confirm that I am once more a ghost."

"Okay…"

Craig reached out and tried to touch Shiro's fingertips. His hand passed through the ghost. Normality, of a kind, had been restored. Along with the usual icy sensation, Craig also got a glimpse of Shiro's mind. It was like gazing into a bottomless pit of misery. No normal man could have endured such self-reproach, regret, and shame.

"My soul is weighed down so that I cannot escape a world that has long since forgotten me," Shiro said. "A great mountain crushes a songbird, yet the songbird still dreams of flight. I humbly request your assistance to free my spirit."

So that's it, Craig thought.

"You need all three of us to help you move on," he said. "All that rigmarole leads up to this."

Shiro bowed curtly.

"That is so."

Tara snorted.

"You've got a damn strange way of asking a favor," she said. "Why should we help you?"

The ghost put his hands together as in prayer.

"I had no choice. The *kami*, one of the most ancient and strange of its kind, insisted on an ordeal to test you."

"Why?" Shane demanded.

Shiro turned to him and bowed.

"The motives of the *kami* remain obscure to me. It is not for mortals or ghosts to question such beings. I only know that I was promised merciful oblivion if I fulfilled its wishes. And it has conferred great gifts upon you, has it not?"

"Do we get to keep them?" Shane asked.

Shiro did not reply. He seemed to be listening to a voice the living could not hear.

"No," he said finally. "They will fade over time. Within one cycle of the moon, they will be gone."

Shane muttered something under his breath.

"Better than nothing," Tara observed coldly. "But it's kind of a shitty bargain."

Craig stepped forward and gave Shiro what he hoped was a graceful bow.

"Is there anything else you can tell us about Sanagi, his followers, or the idol of Yelbeghen?"

"Yes," the ghost said. "And all will be told if you help me end this existence, which is a torment. You will know the truth of my defeat and disgrace, so far as any man can know truth. And you will see Sanagi."

Craig heard voices behind him in the alley. Someone might interrupt them at any moment.

"Let's move him on," he said.

Everyone stood staring at each other for a moment.

"How the hell do we do it?" Shane asked.

Craig had already begun thinking about that. Psychokinesis was relatively simple by comparison. This was, essentially, ghost-wrangling with a team. An old idea, cliched and discredited by a thousand ghost stories, came to him. And it seemed right.

"I think we should link hands."

CHAPTER 19

WHEN THE BLACK SHIPS CAME

Craig closed his eyes and reached out for other spirits. He found three, two glowing with a strange brightness different from any spirit he had encountered. They were spirits still of the living. Tara and Shane. His brain did its best to render them as things of light, Shane blue-white and intense; Tara, a more subdued gold. With these images came something else. Thoughts, feelings, fleeting hints of two very different personalities.

He glimpsed Tara's life, fragmentary and jumbled, its events out of order. He saw werewolves, huge and slavering with rapacious hunger. He shared her terror and courage as she fought a pale, demonic creature that collected the souls of children. And he tried to grasp something else, a baffling encounter in a graveyard. A rendezvous that seemed at once weirdly sexual and also murderous.

Possessed, he thought. *She was possessed.*

Craig recoiled, ashamed by his unintentional voyeurism. He made a conscious effort not to look at the harsher light that was Shane.

"Okay, guys. Focus. Follow me in."

Craig visualized his spirit moving toward Shiro, entangling itself with the essence of the long-dead samurai. He felt the others nearby. Tara was too hesitant, and Shane was too aggressive. The idea was to work as a team, but they were pulling in different directions. Shiro was shying away from Shane, and Tara was not really in the game. Shiro's spirit, a smoky orange light, retreated and dwindled.

"Shiro, trust me," Craig said. "We can do this. I promise. Courage!"

The warrior's soul became stronger, and its light brightened. Craig reached out and urged the others to follow suit. He focused on moving Shiro on and sensed the opening of a portal above them. The process was challenging. Something bound Shiro to this place more strongly than a normal ghost. It was shame. The sense of humiliation that no samurai could bear. Shiro's death had been a bad one, and he would have to face that before his spirit could move on.

Shane and Tara were getting the hang of it now. He sensed Shane's raw power, and Tara's more subtle skill giving his wild talent a boost. He opened his eyes to see a swirling vortex of pale green light. The portal gradually widened until the landscape was revealed. A mountain above a valley. A winding river. A castle on a crag, perched like some great hawk above a town at sunset. Columns of smoke arose from dozens of hearths and a scattering of bakeries and forges.

It was an idyllic vision, and Craig knew without effort that this was Shiro's home. Far to the south, on the island of Shikoku, Shiro had been born and raised in a poor but noble family. His paradise was the old Japan, sealed off from the world. A realm that was impoverished and backward, but stable and at peace. A timeless land of lords and peasants. Craig knew this heavenly recollection would be marred by change of the most violent sort.

Sure enough, the scene shifted to a coast, and a boy called Shiro stood with his father, looking out at smears of smoke on the horizon. A small crowd had gathered on the headland. The foreigners were coming, again, in the latest of many expeditions. More demands on the Shogun. More strange nations of white men with bizarre costumes and flamboyant banners. Their ships moved against the wind and bore weapons no Japanese had seen. Great iron guns that could demolish any castle in minutes. The Shogun was powerless against them.

The crowd muttered a phrase, no one speaking aloud, the same way no one would use a demon's name for fear of summoning it. Everyone spoke of this new, strange force that could not be defied, only appeased.

The Black Ships. The Black Ships.

Shiro's father turned away, his face a picture of desolation. Later, Shiro the man would understand that expression. He, too, would feel that all the old certainties were replaced by some new and terrible chaos. The scene shifted jerkily, jumping back and forth. No human remembers sequentially, and Craig had seen this many times, but he sensed Tara and Shane recoiling from the bizarre experience. It was a baptism of fire for them.

"Hang in there," he said. "It'll settle down."

It did, to a degree. Shiro grew up during a time of turmoil, still learning the way of warrior, the code of bushido. At the same time, rival factions the length of the empire were equipping themselves with foreign weapons. The Shogun, shown to be powerless, was soon overthrown. Black Ships arrived with consignments of weapons for warring factions. Companies of riflemen shot down the samurai of rebellious lords.

Shiro asked his father what he should do, and his father had no answer. Turning from his home, Shiro set off on the road to the capital with vague ideas of seeking his fortune. More confused memories, but this time linked together by a face. A smooth, hairless visage with keen, unblinking eyes. A small man, dressed in the robes of a Shinto priest, standing by the roadside, ranting against foreigners, change, and the barbaric world beyond Japan.

Sanagi.

Craig felt the intensity of the man's spell. He brought a kind of solace. He told his followers that the fault lay with the politicians, merchants, and cowards in the capital. And, of course, with the foreigners, the filthy meat-eating barbarians who had besmirched this land of the gods. Sanagi said the *kami* were angry with the people for not resisting the outsiders. The spirits who safeguarded the people would turn their backs on them. Sanagi prophesied a time when Japan would be devoid of spirituality, in thrall to the foreign cult of greed. It would become a degraded land of bandits and whores and golden sepulchers, paying tribute to the stinking, jabbering monkey men from beyond the sea.

Part of Shiro knew this was insane, that nobody could have sunk the Black Ships. Yet, all his learning and instinct was with Sanagi. And when his new father, his spiritual father, told him to kill, he killed. He slew those who sought to compromise with the outsiders. He slaughtered unnamed men, murdered victims in their sleep, and waylaid merchants and scholars. He terrorized those building railways and factories, and those seeking to open schools of foreign learning.

The Sanagi cult, no more than a few dozen strong, rampaged across the southern provinces. The new government sent police and soldiers after them, but they hid among the people. For every member, a hundred households sympathized with their cause. And then there were those too scared to turn them in.

It made no difference. Years passed, and Japan changed. The smoke of factories and locomotives cast a pall over Shiro's hometown. The Meiji Emperor's fleet darkened the horizon with the smoke of its engines. Troops in Western uniforms drilled on barrack squares and marched through towns to bands playing newly wrought tunes on foreign instruments. Railroads linked the growing cities.

One day, Sanagi called his followers together and admitted that they could not succeed. He told his dwindling band that the *kami* were not with them. The great leader proclaimed that he had been wrong to fight modernization. Of course, they cried out, "No, master, you are never wrong." But Sanagi, after waiting for silence to fall once more, repeated his self-denunciation.

"Yes, my children, I was wrong," he insisted. "Wrong to use the weapons of men to fight men. The weapons of gods, ghosts, and demons shall be ours from now on. We will find allies elsewhere, mortal and immortal. My powers have revealed to me a powerful being who lies dormant, over the sea to the West. I will seek out this being and bring him back so that he may aid us. With his help, we will bring down this reign of the traitors who surrendered our land to foreign barbarians."

And then Sanagi left, without another word, taking just a handful of his most devoted servants. The remaining cultists, now no more than a dozen, pondered their fates. For the first time in years, Shiro began to have doubts. He could not reconcile the paradox of Sanagi seeking help abroad when they aimed to rid Japan of outside influences. Had the enlightened one, the great leader, become deluded?

Shiro kept his opinions to himself at first. Eventually, he blurted out his questions to others as they continued to evade the new regime, and that sealed Shiro's fate. Craig and the others saw a man lying on a futon in a lamplit room, his body oddly contorted. It was Shiro, seen by his ghost. From the ceiling, tiny droplets of liquid fell slowly, as if in slow motion, and caught the lamplight for a moment. Craig was puzzled at first, and then Shiro's understanding became his.

Shiro had been sleeping in a room with its windows and doors barred against assassins. He had not quite resolved to surrender to the government. In his mental turmoil, he had overlooked one vulnerability: the attic. One of the cultists had removed a ceiling panel and dangled an almost invisible thread until its end hung just above Shiro's face as he slept. Drops of poison, lethal even in tiny amounts, had been poured onto the thread and descended onto the sleeper's face. It only took one drop to reach Shiro's lips, and it was over.

A shameful death. A traitor's death. Slain in the night while my katana lay sheathed by my side.

In shared memory, Craig followed Shiro's ghost from the room, and into the night of old Tokyo. He saw that the samurai had died just yards from the *torii* they had all passed through. The *kami* of the shrine had bound Shiro to its purpose. The *kami* spoke to the ghost of a time when strangers would come. More than a century must pass before a sacred ordeal could be undertaken. Only the strangers' arrival could free Shiro and let him pass on to the afterlife.

I wish to leave now.

Craig was back in the present. The portal above them was wide, and the vista beyond it was inviting.

"Where is Sanagi? Where is the idol?"

Shiro was rising, his face no longer depressed but smiling in anticipation.

"Shiro, you promised, dammit!"

The ghost spoke without looking back.

"Seek the village of the dead."

CHAPTER 20
FIRST NIGHT

"Well, I'm absolutely cream-crackered."

Tara flung herself backward onto the huge bed. To his credit, Stark had booked them into a splendid midtown hotel. Their room was on the fourteenth floor, with a massive window that looked out over the city. The vast metropolis was a work of art in pulsing neon and moving headlights. Looking down at the darkened streets, Craig wondered who or what might be looking back at him. He thought of the slit-mouthed woman and shuddered.

"At least we've got decent AC," he said, reaching for a positive.

Tara made a plaintive noise.

"Too little, too late! Humidity at nearly a hundred percent; that's not good. And the air pollution is bad, too. We should get out of Tokyo as soon as possible and find this village of the dead."

Despite being exhausted, the team had discussed Shiro's message on the way back to the hotel. They hadn't reached an agreement. Shane thought Tokyo's ghosts might offer more information. Craig was skeptical, seeing how standoffish and self-absorbed most local ghosts appeared.

Tara was leaning toward Craig's point of view. As she had pointed out, Stark had given them some local contacts—living ones—and the weapons guy in Tokyo. There was also a retired professor in Kyoto who was an expert on cults and the supernatural. Shane was not so impressed by academics.

"Maybe we should split up," Craig mused. "Shane's kind of a lone wolf. That's how he's used to working. It can't be easy keeping an eye out for us. He can't help seeing us as sidekicks, and it's a fair point guess. And he's got enhanced powers now, so…"

Tara sighed.

"He will do what he likes; I know. Just let me lie here and simmer for a while. My brain stopped working an hour ago."

"Okay," Craig said, "I'll see if I can figure out the high-tech shower."

The bathroom was bright, spotlessly clean, and futuristic. Craig studied the control panel by the toilet. He tried one button, and it played a chirpy pop tune that might have been called elevator music under different circumstances. The idea was to drown out embarrassing sounds.

"You doing karaoke in there?" Tara shouted.

"Sorry!"

Deciding not to improvise further, Craig got his phone and used a handy app to translate as much as he could. As well as music or white noise, the toilet offered him the option of a heated seat. This, he didn't need. Then, there was a small tube that emerged from under the rim to squirt water for cleansing purposes. The bidet had a temperature control. Craig wondered how many unwary tourists had scalded themselves, and how many had dared to admit it.

The shower was much simpler, for which Craig was thankful. He decided to begin with that. As he stood under the refreshing deluge, he reflected on the fact that he was in a country infested with supernatural beings. This was a society devoted to modern technology, or at least it seemed so from a tourist perspective. Then, he wondered what a newcomer to his country might think of the U.S. Just as weird, he guessed, if not more so.

Every land is a land of contrasts, he concluded.

Having showered, he tackled the challenge of the toilet and emerged unscathed. Tara asked how it was, and he struggled to find appropriate words. This produced some hilarity, and Craig realized that they had managed to relax. Tara showered and emerged, looking refreshed and wrapped in a smallish towel. Craig turned his back as she got dressed for bed.

"So, you're sure you don't need anything more than painkillers?" he asked. "We could go to a pharmacist; they're open all hours here."

"Nah," she said, "I feel a lot better. I mean, I'm going to sleep like a log, but otherwise, it's just a few bruises. And the shock, of course. That tongue thing really caught me a wallop. I owe you one for that. And the other stuff."

Craig was standing by the window again. The city was fascinating like some great work of modern art grown insanely large. In the distance, he saw the Tokyo Tower. It was a replica of the Eiffel Tower but painted red and white, Japan's national colors. He wondered what French tourists made of it. Mentioning this to Tara, she surprised him with a reply.

"There's a fake Statue of Liberty in Yokohama, and another one in Osaka, I think. You can turn around now; I'm decent. Well, decent as I'll ever be."

"You look great," he said.

She collapsed back onto the bed, wearing an oversized T-shirt and loose shorts. He felt the urge to lie down beside her and smooch, but were they at the smooching stage? They had kissed hastily a couple of times. Craig tried to recall if they had set any boundaries but was fuzzy on the topic.

"Guess I'll put up our defenses," he said, changing the subject in his head. "No, don't help; you need to rest. Seriously. You took a hit, I didn't."

He did his best to encircle the bed with iron filings and a band of salt. They had also brought some Japanese charms against ghosts and other entities. These small scrolls bore ancient incantations. Craig put them at the cardinal points around the bed. For good measure, he placed more charms by the doors and windows.

"They'll charge us a small fortune for cleaning the room," he said sadly. "I hate to get a bad rep with such nice people. Is there some way we can clean it up?"

"We can get one of those teeny, cheap vacuum cleaners." Tara was checking her phone. "There's a big discount store nearby. Don Quixote. Always with the weird names! Anyway, I'll put it on tomorrow's to-do list."

Craig sat on the bed. Sheer exhaustion, both mental and physical, was starting to show. She looked up at him, frowning slightly.

"You know, that dipper bothers me. Maybe more than it should."

"Why?" he asked.

"It seemed kind of convenient." She closed her eyes and wriggled into a comfier position. "Normally, a dipper at a shrine would be made of wood, or partly wooden, at least. Didn't that whole setup feel like a game? Passing through the gateway. Encountering a series of threats. Using an improvised weapon…"

Craig mulled it over for a moment, and a thought struck him.

"And powering up. We powered up, didn't we? Gained new abilities."

Tara opened her eyes and looked at him seriously.

"Uh-huh, just like a game. Which is appropriate, I guess, given we're in Japan. Supernatural beings everywhere play games and pose riddles, that kind of thing."

Craig tried to form coherent thoughts about their ordeal, but his exhaustion made it hard to think. He lay down beside Tara and felt lethargy weigh on him like lead. He felt her hand close on his, but even a gentle smooch now seemed unlikely. Still, it felt good to be with Tara, and this sudden sharing of their abilities was oddly comforting. Even if it wore off in a few weeks, they were almost one entity for the time being.

Along with Shane, of course.

Craig was too tired to think anymore. Sleep overtook him, and the sound of the AC faded along with the dimly lit room. He awoke after what seemed like a split second to feel Tara's hand still holding his. He gave her fingers a gentle squeeze, which was returned.

But something felt wrong. The room was brighter. Craig turned his head and saw a thin, white line near the floor. A light was coming from under the bathroom door. As he stared in confusion, the door opened and Tara appeared, pushing her hair back from her face. A flushing sound came from behind her, partly masked by a jaunty little tune.

Tara shuffled forward a few paces and stopped. Craig saw a black smear on the carpet behind her. For a second, he didn't grasp what it might be. Then, he thought of iron filings.

"Aw, I'm sorry," Tara said. "Did I wake you?"

Craig sat up, twisted around, and looked down to see a familiar face smiling up at him more widely than anyone had the right to. He struggled to get free, but it was futile. The grotesque interloper clutched him even tighter, crushing his fingers in a grip that was suddenly icy.

The slit-mouthed woman spoke.

"Am I beautiful?"

"No!" he yelled without thinking.

He saw a gleam of metal before the scissors plunged into his right eye and pain exploded inside his skull.

CHAPTER 21

THE WOMAN WITH SCISSORS

She can't kill me, she can't kill me...

Craig repeated it like a mantra in his head. He didn't die when she stabbed him in the eye, so he confirmed the *yokai* indeed couldn't kill him.

He was grappling with the red-clad woman, failing to overcome her inhuman strength. She pulled the scissors out of his right eye and stabbed at his left. He jerked his head to one side so that the blade pierced his ear. More pain, but not too much, more like manageable agony. Some vestiges of logic surfaced and told him to rethink his tactics. He gave up on pushing her away. They were close; maybe getting closer would help. He yielded to her, letting her pull him up against her. The *yokai* pressed her mutilated mouth against his cheek.

"So young, so cute," she murmured. "Be mine forever!"

The last word was emphasized with a piercing spasm of pain in his nape. More blows followed as she plunged her oversized scissors into his back, his skull, and his shoulders. The speed with which she could strike was terrifying. He was not bleeding; there were no actual cuts, but the damage was still accumulating. Shock alone could knock him out, especially in his exhausted state.

"Get off him, you bitch!"

Tara's scream coincided with a sudden stiffening of the *yokai*. The slit-mouthed woman let out a gurgling bellow that suggested pain mingled with surprise. She slackened her grip on Craig, and he seized the opportunity to break free. He tried to get to his feet but instead found himself slumping to the floor. Tara was standing over him, in the act of throwing something.

Iron filings, he realized. The small glass vial of black powder was almost empty.

Craig hauled himself upright in time to see the evil spirit spring up from the bed and leap toward Tara. The medical scissors slashed down, and Tara was too slow. The blades went deep into her shoulder, and she screamed. The *yokai* grabbed her and reprised her attack on Craig, holding Tara close and driving her weapon into Tara's back. Craig lunged forward and grabbed at the red kimono, but the sheer silk was impossible to hold onto tightly.

Brooch, he thought. *Where is it?*

As if in reply, Tara's iron brooch rose into the air from the bedside table. It flew erratically. Its owner was in too much pain to control it precisely. Craig reached out with his mind and guided the brooch into the back of the *yokai.* It was not moving very fast, but the impact had an effect. The slit-mouthed woman stopped stabbing Tara and shoved her away. Tara fell heavily as the *yokai* turned and grinned down at Craig.

"Am I beautiful?"

"About average!" he shouted in desperation as he shuffled away from her on his ass.

"No, that will not do!"

The hideous creature advanced, scissors raised to stab down at her prey. Craig felt something under his right hand. Paper? Then he recalled the charms at the corners of the bed. He grasped the small scroll, wondering if it might have some effect. The *yokai* seized on his hesitation to pounce, lunging forward and down. The ghostly scissors entered the top of his head. Another piercing jolt of pain, and he almost passed out. His vision blurred, and he wanted to throw up.

"What the hell—"

It was Shane's voice. Beyond the *yokai,* Craig saw blurred movement. A struggle was underway. For the moment, the hideous interloper was pinioned. As Craig struggled to get upright, his vision cleared, and he saw

Shane and Tara grappling with the grinning monstrosity.

Even as Craig regained his footing, a sweeping blow from a kimono-clad arm sent Tara spinning away, leaving Shane battling alone. They were all too tired, Craig realized, drained by their previous encounter. They simply could not match the power of the *yokai*, even working together.

Craig decided to try something that was probably stupid. He was unsteady on his feet, in pain, and scared. It was the time for desperate measures. But he could just remember what the scrolls signified. No supernatural entity could go near them. They repelled occult forces.

Craig turned away for a moment so the *yokai* wouldn't see what he was doing, then stepped forward. Instead of grabbing the creature, he spoke calmly to her.

"You are beautiful," he said. "Please, grant me one kiss before I die."

The *yokai's* eyes widened. Shane, maintaining a chokehold on the horror, looked startled, too.

"Let her go, Shane," Craig insisted confidently. "She is beautiful, and I must die in her embrace."

Shane, still unsure of Craig's plan but trusted he had one, released his grip on the *yokai*.

"Very well," the slit-mouthed woman said. "I cannot refuse such a request."

"Craig!" Tara shouted. "Wait!"

Craig leaned toward the hideous creature and forced himself to press his lips to her mutilated mouth. The flesh was cold and dry. He reached out and took her head with his hands to prolong the kiss. Her arms clutched him closer, so tightly he felt sure a rib would crack. Then, he spat the scroll into her mouth. He clenched his jaw as she began to writhe and emit muffled screams. She broke free in just a few seconds, but by that time, the ancient charm had done some damage.

The woman's face darkened, and her traditional pale makeup was replaced by patches of rotting flesh. Puffs of blue-gray smoke emerged from her screaming mouth. Chunks of flesh fell away from her face to reveal brownish-yellow bone. What had been delicate, graceful fingers were now bony talons with yellow, ragged nails. Even the red kimono faded, becoming threadbare and torn. The slit-mouthed woman gagged and tried to spit out the scroll, but it was too late. The ancient characters had wrought their magic. They were burned into her tongue.

The stench of decay filled the air and again, Craig nearly puked. Then, the *yokai* collapsed, transformed in moments from a formidable foe into little more than a heap of rags and bones. A face that was more skull than flesh gazed at Craig. The *yokai's* voice, previously strong and seductive, now sounded weak.

"I have known better kissers."

Then all that was left of the clash was the scroll, lying crumpled on the hotel carpet. Craig bent to pick it up. The thin parchment was damp and stained with something that smelled bad. He dropped the scroll.

"Maybe we can make do with three," he muttered and sat heavily on the bed.

Shane sat next to Craig and gave him a not-too-gentle punch on the arm.

"If that hadn't worked, we'd have all been screwed. I mean, it was smart. I bet nobody's ever tried to kiss her before."

Tara had struggled onto a chair and was sitting opposite them. She looked bedraggled and confused.

"How did she get through in the first place, though?"

"You were in the shower. I thought you came out, we talked, and you hopped onto bed," Craig recounted. "I told you not to worry, that I'd add the protection barrier myself. But it was her the entire time."

Shane grasped the situation at once.

"Tired people make mistakes. Saw that too many times in the Corps and outside. Solution? Get some rest. And don't beat yourself up over one screwup. Okay, we get you guys set up with effective barriers again, and this time, I'll stay up on the couch, in case another *yokai* shows up."

It took them a lot longer to restore the barrier around the bed, but they got it done. Tara would not brook any shortcuts. Given that the scroll had survived its encounter with the *yokai*, they voted unanimously to put it back on sentry duty. It was well after midnight by the time she declared they were ready for shuteye.

Now that the adrenalin had stopped pumping, Craig was overwhelmed with fatigue. But, as time passed, it became obvious that he couldn't sleep. Tara, in contrast, was already snoring gently at his side. Craig tried a few tricks to fall asleep, but none worked. He turned his head to look at Shane, who raised a hand in a maybe-ironic "okay" gesture. Craig managed a weak smile.

And then, without warning, he sank into a dreamless sleep.

CHAPTER 22
AKIHABARA

The trio was rested the next morning but still jet-lagged and far from tip-top condition. But two of them had an appointment. And, as Shane observed, if you have an appointment to get some weapons, you always keep it. As Stark was—they hoped—ignorant of Shane's involvement, though, they would have to part ways for a few hours. Shane would continue his quest to get information from Tokyo's ghosts.

Craig and Tara took a taxi to Akihabara, a tourist-heavy district famous for rip-off prices. It seemed apt that Stark's operative would meet them there. The guy, who used the name Sora, had sent them a series of texts with limited information on his exact whereabouts. It seemed that Sora was a little paranoid and wanted to scope them out first.

So it was that the two found themselves standing outside a store that seemed to stock every possible anime-related product. A mostly young, mostly Japanese crowd flocked past them, many toting branded clothing or boxed action figures. The bewildering array of anime characters reminded Craig of the plethora of *yokai*, *kami*, and other strange entities. It seemed that, whenever Japan produced anything weird, real, or fictitious, it went in for mass production.

"Yeah, I guess. There are supposed to be eight million *kami*," Tara said when Craig mentioned this to her.

"No way," Craig responded. "I mean, that would be eight million shrines…"

Tara shook her head.

"More research needed, buddy. A *kami* isn't just a being worshipped at a shrine. It can be a mountain, a river, or even a living person."

She went on to explain that a Japanese demon, or *oni*, often begins as a horrible human being. Craig looked at the passing throng and wondered if any of the fresh-faced kids with their colorful purchases might be demons in the making. It seemed unlikely, but Craig had the impression that almost anything unlikely might still happen in Japan.

"This country is nuts," he blurted out, then reddened at the thought that someone might have overheard. "I mean, it's confusing as all get out. But fascinating."

Tara laughed.

"Remember, very few people speak English, and even if they do, they're not going to confront you about a remark like that. It would draw attention to *them*. Making a fuss is heinous. Loss of face. It's basically a nation of anti-Karens."

She seemed about to deliver another short lecture on local culture when she paused to look at her phone again.

"Okay, right. Our guy says we can come on up. He sent a picture of the building... oh."

She held up her phone.

"It's a maid café, isn't it?" Craig asked before even looking. "It couldn't be a Starbucks or a pharmacy."

"But at least this one isn't cat-themed. Probably."

They walked a few hundred yards to a building whose entrance was flanked by brightly colored posters. The overall look offered a distinct overdose of cuteness. A Japanese girl in a maid outfit greeted them profusely with much smiling, bowing, and hand-heart gestures. She led them upstairs to a fake Victorian doorway surrounded by artificial roses. Another two young maids appeared and proceeded to "welcome home" what they called "our lord and lady". Being welcomed back to a place he'd never been made Craig cringe inwardly. Still far from acclimatized, he felt this might be a dream that could suddenly turn into a nightmare.

"Seems like we've got to go through with it," Tara whispered. "But it's a good way to let Stark's guy check us out."

She gave a significant look toward a security camera above the café counter.

"I wish it wasn't so—cringey," Craig grumbled.

"Like you're not enjoying yourself," Tara remarked as the maids led them to a table.

"I'm not!" he protested.

Despite it not being 10 AM yet, there were people at two other tables. One party appeared to be middle-aged European tourists with a local guide. The others were nerdy-looking young Japanese guys. Neither group looked even slightly suspect to Craig. Overheard snatches of conversation seemed authentically banal, and, in the case of the tourists, a wee bit creepy.

"So, do you feel really awkward?" he asked Tara as they took their seats.

No reply.

"Okay, just me then."

It seemed that they had to go through the whole experience. Tara got another message from Sora. She frowned.

"Problem?" Craig asked.

Tara shrugged.

"The message seems a little weird. Kind of half-assed."

She passed the phone over. Under "Sora" was the phrase "watch out". Nothing else.

"That's what I'd call unhelpful," he said, handing back Tara's phone.

Watch out for what? he thought.

Craig tried to discreetly observe the other customers and again saw nothing sketchy. The maids were now performing a little song and dance routine with the Japanese guys. Along with the café's pink and powder-blue décor, a less dangerous place would be hard to imagine.

"Maybe Sora's paranoid," he suggested. "He's got plenty to be paranoid about. Helping foreigners to steal the Sanagi cult's idol is high-risk stuff."

A maid approached their table and asked if they would like to order. It seemed they had to go through the rigmarole of being regular customers. Anyway, they had skipped breakfast after getting up a little late. Tara suggested something called omurice, so Craig went along with it. The result was an omelet over a layer of rice that tasted surprisingly good.

"Do you think Sora is checking with Stark?" he asked.

"Maybe," Tara said, "but we're being asked to take a lot on trust as well. We had a narrow escape last time we met one of these subcontractors."

Craig thought back to their encounter in London. There, Stark's man provided the team with weapons and other gear, only to nearly die due to a ghost attack. Craig realized belatedly that he was sitting with his back to the entrance and felt a tingle between his shoulder blades. It was irrational, given that ghosts and other entities didn't need to use a doorway, but it summed up the situation. The café was excessively cute in appearance and general atmosphere, but it was that very fakeness that made Craig wonder what might lie behind the façade.

Time passed, and there were no further messages. They'd finished eating and were sipping sodas when the maid who'd first welcomed them leaned over Craig's shoulder.

"Sora will be pleased to see you now." The girl smiled sweetly. "He is on the next floor, green door."

She looked upward and winked.

They paid a surprisingly small amount for the food. Tara insisted that they behave like regular tourists, so they also had their pictures taken with the maids for an extra fee that only added to the surreal feeling. Craig wondered if he would ever get used to Tokyo and its bizarre combination of ancient and modern, fantasy and reality.

Outside, they took the stairs to the top floor. It consisted of more cafés and bars, most themed in some way. All were closed at this time of day. One purported to be an American diner; another, a British-style pub. Tara lingered at the latter, scanning the list of beers, then reluctantly moved along.

"Sudden dose of nostalgia," she grinned. "I could murder a pint right now, as they say. Hey, there's the green door. Must be our guy."

Craig agreed. It was the only premise with no sign outside. There was simply a number, 42. Above the green door was another security camera. Craig gave a quick peace sign as they stopped and waited for a response. When there was no sign of life after about ten seconds, Craig pushed the intercom buzzer. Someone spoke after a crackle.

"Were you followed?"

"No," Craig responded.

"What about the bald guy at your hotel? You are supposed to keep a low profile."

That was disconcerting. Someone—or perhaps something—had seen them with Shane. Fortunately, they had a simple cover story ready. Tara took over.

"That was just a boring American guy who sat next to us on the plane. We didn't realize he'd be at the same hotel. We had to shake him off."

A pause. Then the speaker crackled again.

"Very well. You may enter."

CHAPTER 23
STARK'S GUY IN TOKYO

Sora's lair was bathed in shadows thanks to indirect lighting. If there was a window, Craig thought, it must be hidden behind one of the numerous cupboards, cabinets, or fully laden shelves. They made a tight space seem even smaller. It seemed that Sora was a hoarder. Almost every square inch of space was covered with heaps of newspapers and magazines. There was a narrow pathway between the entrance and the back of the store.

"Are you sure you weren't followed?"

Peering into the gloom, Craig could just make out a person seated at a desk. To each side of Sora was a screen, angled away from the newcomers. Their blue glow was all that revealed the man's presence.

"We weren't followed," Tara said. "We took all the precautions you asked us to."

Sora stood. He was not tall by Western standards, but a good height for a Japanese. He stepped forward and revealed a youthful face under a mop of long, floppy blond hair. Sora wore a T-shirt with *The Clash—London Calling* emblazoned across the front, complete with a black-and-white photo of the band.

"Nice undercut," Tara observed.

It took Craig a second to grasp she meant Sora's hairstyle.

"Thanks," the Japanese man said, unsmiling, "but Stark is paying me to equip you guys, not make conversation. I got as much stuff together as I could. Let's get started."

Sora reached behind his desk and produced, one by one, an impressive array of weapons. He had iron shuriken and iron daggers. Craig had always thought throwing stars only existed in movies, but it seemed they were real. He turned one over in his hand, wincing as a point pricked his index finger.

"You need training to use them effectively," Sora remarked, "but they're compact and easy to hide. And I guess you could practice on a tree or whatever if you're out in the countryside."

Craig almost mentioned their psychokinetic powers, but he bit his tongue. Stark had likely given Sora the bare minimum information. Craig had to resist the temptation to brag about his newfound ability. Giving in to such an immature impulse could put them all in danger.

"You okay?" Sora asked with a shrewd look.

"Fine," Craig said. "You're right; we should practice with those things."

Satisfied, Sora moved on to longer-range weapons.

"You've got options." He opened a small crate. "Just a reminder that firearms are permanently off the agenda in his country, so it's small-sized crossbows, BB guns, or both."

"Crossbows are harder to conceal from the cops." Craig picked up an air pistol.

Tara, who had been examining a crossbow, handed it back to Sora.

"I guess so," she said sadly. "How about concealment, anyway?"

"Yep. Got you covered."

Sora picked his way through the labyrinth of trash and produced an ordinary-looking wheeled suitcase. He placed it on his desk and opened it.

"False bottom," he explained, sliding a deft hand down inside the case. "There's a trick to it."

With a faint click, the secret compartment was revealed and contained two black plastic cases designed to attach to a belt. Sora explained that these were tasers. The case was roomy enough to also house two pistols and a supply of iron pellets, plus a couple of daggers. Thinking of Shane, Craig asked if Sora had any spare weapons. Sora shrugged and produced another knife.

"These are all forged in Sakai, down Osaka way," he said as Tara studied the dagger. "Best quality craftsmanship, though iron blades like this are always a special commission. That's why I don't buy many—it draws too much interest. I can only let you have this one spare."

That would have to do. Craig had been coached in hand-to-hand combat and the use of weapons by Tara since their last mission. He could at least shoot straight. Kind of. Hefting one of the pistols, he asked how effective iron pellets might be against *yokai*.

"Depends. Some will be destroyed, but they're the little guys—mischief-makers; not really a threat. Hell, some might even help you if they feel like it. The tasers might be helpful against them, too."

"What about the ones that aren't little guys?"

Sora smiled for the first time.

"Physical weapons might slow the real monsters enough for you to escape, or you might just piss them off, and they'll come at your even harder."

Great, Craig thought.

He slipped the pistol into the secret compartment alongside the other weapons. Sora closed the false bottom and then the case.

"I guess we'll need more occult protection, then," Tara looked around. "You've got a lot of cool stuff here; there must be something effective."

Sora wove his way through the paper maze again and returned with a plastic container. Inside, there was a jumble of items of various sizes and shapes. He opened the box and scooped out a handful of small brocade bags.

"*Onamori*," he explained. "Amulets against evil. Each bag contains a parchment or small wooden board with a special incantation written by a monk or priest. Evil beings are repelled by these things, even harmed in some cases."

Craig nodded as he thought of the scroll he'd used on the slit-mouthed woman.

"Which ones are the best?" He examined a bag made of dark red velvet.

Sora shrugged.

"These are all decent quality, not just tourist stuff. All the big names in Shinto and Buddhism endorse the product."

Craig tried not to smile at what sounded very much like a sales pitch. He put the bag into his back pocket.

"Okay, we'll just take an assortment. But you must have something a bit, you know, stronger? Stark said you were the main man for paranormal stuff."

Sora gazed at Craig speculatively before vanishing among the shelves. They heard rummaging sounds, a clink of glass, and then the clink of metal. Finally, the young man returned carrying a saucer-shaped object about four inches across.

"Frisbee?" Tara asked.

Sora gave another humorless smile.

"This is a *makyo*," he said. "A kind of bronze mirror, originally from China. This one's more than a thousand years old, and it's unique. Nobody ever made a *makyo* like it. Stark was very specific about you having this. Cost a fricking fortune."

Sora held up the metal disk. It was unimpressive in the poor light. It had a slightly concave surface on which some kind of pattern was engraved.

"What does it do?" Craig asked.

Sora went to his desk and flicked on a lamp. Craig, dazzled by the sudden light, couldn't see what Sora was up to. Then, he grasped that the man had angled the mirror so it was reflecting the lamplight onto the ceiling. He looked up. The mirror was projecting an image. Sora wasn't holding the mirror completely steady, and the circular pattern wobbled and went out of focus. Then it sharpened again, and Craig could see it showed a seven-headed creature.

"Yelbeghen!"

"Yeah, the big guy," Sora said flatly. "Total bastard from what I heard. But keep watching. See if it happens again. I tried it out earlier; it's a cool phenomenon."

After a few baffled moments, Craig saw what the other man meant. The image was not static. The beast moved, waving its fearsome heads and flailing immense limbs and a tail.

"Moving pictures!" Tara breathed.

As if on cue, the projected image froze, and Yelbeghen was once again just a regular engraving, albeit a superbly detailed one.

Sora handed the mirror to Craig, who was surprised at its lightness.

"It's impressive," he conceded, "but what use is it to us?"

"The closer you are to the genuine article, the more it moves," Sora explained. "That's the theory, anyway. See how it only moved for a second? Yelbeghen isn't close, but he's probably somewhere on this island. That's how I read it, anyhow. There's some other stuff in the old books, but it's mostly nonsense. One thing that might be true, though, is that it has some kind of prophetic power."

Sora seemed set to say more but was interrupted by a loud buzzer. Frowning, he squeezed past his clients and went to the door. A conversation over the intercom ensued. It seemed that the person outside had a message that had to be delivered in person. Craig thought he recognized the voice of the maid who'd shown them up.

"I can't talk out here!" the girl insisted in Japanese. "Please let me in! It's important!"

Craig walked over to the desk, fascinated by the mirror, and projected the image onto the ceiling. The seven-headed beast appeared, blurry and unmoving. Then, Craig's attention was caught by one of the computer screens. It was showing a live feed from the camera above Sora's shop door. The girl in the maid outfit was just visible, and Craig could see the top of her head and her eyes. She glanced up, not at the camera but past it. At something on the ceiling, maybe. When they'd first met her, she'd been the epitome of cuteness, but not now. Her face was a mask of fear. Then, something blocked the camera, moving swiftly in front of the lens.

Craig turned toward Sora just as he heard the distinctive buzz and click of the door being unlocked.

"No!" he yelled.

But it was too late.

CHAPTER 24
NIGHTMARE FUEL

Japanese doors opened outward. That had struck Craig as odd when he found out. Now, when Sora looked back at him as the door of Unit 42 swung out into the corridor, a quirky cultural difference became a matter of life and death. Something vast, dark, and many-legged descended from above the doorway, and it was impossible to shut it out. The maid café girl screamed and ran off down the corridor. When Craig got a better look at the creature, he understood her point of view.

But he and Tara had nowhere to run.

The entity was like a vast, white spider. It was covered in coarse grayish hair but had a face that—while far larger than any man's—looked approximately human. The main difference was the eyes: eight of them in four pairs, stacked one atop the other. Strands of gray web descended around the monster as it landed and then braced itself to jump. Realizing his mistake, Sora leaped sideways but stumbled over one of the ubiquitous heaps of garbage. The spider thing struggled briefly in the doorway, eager to get at the man but too unwieldy in its hairy bulk to easily fit through the narrow gap.

Sora seized the brief respite to get up and sprint toward the Americans. The arachnid reacted with a loud hiss of might have been rage. Then, Craig saw the gray-white strands spurting from either side of the nightmarish head. The semi-liquid filaments seemed possessed, entangling Sora with incredible speed and dragging his legs from under him. He landed heavily, and the crash was shockingly loud in the darkened room.

"Help me! Oh, God, help me!"

Sora reached out, his eyes filled with terror and pleading. Craig ran forward and took his hand, but the spider silk had hardened and now seemed to have the strength of a strong rope. The monster advanced, scuttling on spindly limbs, all the while pulling Sora toward it. Craig shuddered as the creature opened its mouth. What had seemed like a human jaw extended down and outward to reveal huge fangs. Craig didn't doubt that, like an ordinary spider, the thing killed its prey with venom.

"Craig, get down!"

He responded instinctively to Tara's warning as something whizzed over his head. One of the entity's eyes seemed suddenly larger and wept black tears. Craig realized Tara was hurling the *shuriken*. A second iron star flashed by, but this one missed an eye and embedded itself in the parody of a man's face. The monster screeched and thrashed its huge limbs, then yanked viciously on the webbing that imprisoned Sora. Craig lost his grip, and Sora, still yelling for help, was pulled underneath the huge, hairy body. The fangs descended and plunged into Sora's chest.

The man didn't scream for long, but it seemed like an eternity.

Craig ran back to Tara, who had opened the case with the secret compartment and was pulling out an air pistol.

"It's too damn big," Craig cried. "It'll just absorb the damage."

He picked up the mirror and, spinning around, flung it like a frisbee at the creature. He did his best to accelerate it and aim it, but his telekinetic power was erratic, and the bronze disk glanced off the side of the thing's head.

"Try this!" Tara said.

She handed him a dagger and levitated a second. Craig followed suit, and they hurled the iron blades at the monster. Like its smaller brethren, the huge spider could move very fast from a standing start. It managed to dodge Craig's blade, but Tara's cut into the second of its right-hand limbs. More dark fluid sprayed out, and the room again filled with unearthly screeching. Then the creature, abandoning Sora's unmoving form, leaped onto one of the cabinets and was out of sight in a heartbeat.

Tara leveled an air pistol at that side of the room.

"Could we make a run for it?" Craig asked.

The creature might have heard and understood. A loud scrabbling was followed by the toppling of a glass-fronted cabinet. It blocked the doorway, crashing to the floor and scattering its contents plus shards of glass around their escape route. The spider thing was visible for a split second, and Tara got off a shot, but she either missed or it had no effect. Then, the monster scurried out of sight.

Craig looked at the fallen cabinet. They could clamber over it, but it would take precious seconds, and they wouldn't be able to defend themselves. They stood, unsure of what to do next. The monster could not move in the cramped, rubbish-packed space without making noise, but if it came at them, how long would they have to defend themselves? Not long enough.

"Headssss…"

The voice was sibilant, high-pitched, and just barely comprehensible. Craig tried to identify the direction it came from, but it was futile in the dark, cramped space.

"Headsss musssst be taken…"

"Jesus," Tara muttered. "Like it needs to psych us out."

Craig glanced at Sora's body. His head was intact. The monster's taunt was baffling, but perhaps that was the idea. Another surge of movement, and a bookcase fell. This one was closer to them. Again, they got a fleeting glimpse of the entity. This time, they both fired at it, and there was a shriek in response, but the creature showed no signs of slowing down.

"Any ideas?" Tara panted.

Craig racked his brain for anything effective. There were several spider *yokai*, he knew, and all were formidable. The sort of trick he'd played on the slit-mouthed woman wouldn't work. Getting close enough to make a physical attack was impossible, and they had no weapon to strike from a distance.

"But maybe we don't need to." He recalled something Tara had told him about her power.

"What?" Tara looked at him with wide eyes.

Craig spelled out his idea. She raised one obvious objection.

"We're stuck in here with that thing!"

"What other choice—" Craig began, then swore.

Great festoons of spiderweb floated over the remaining cabinets to their left. The pale, sticky strands clung to the pair despite their best efforts to tear them off. The scrabbling sound came again, and the *yokai* appeared, clinging to the ceiling. They raised their pistols to fire, and Tara flung a *shuriken* with her mind. This time, the monster took the hits almost casually, barely flinching as it sprayed out more gray-white filaments.

"We've got to try it!" Craig insisted.

"Okay," Tara hissed. "Focus on the head?"

Craig dug deep and, for only the second time, tried to focus his newfound power. He tried to refine Tara's visualization technique. He had to see what he wanted to move. In this case, though, he wasn't just reaching out with an extra-long arm to give an opponent a shove; he was manipulating matter on a more fundamental level.

"I'm getting there," Tara said with effort. "But come on, help me!"

Craig waved his arms to stop the web filaments from hardening, but it would only work temporarily. He struggled to focus, to imagine the molecules in the monstrous, half-human head. He realized that couldn't do it, so instead, he simply jabbed at the thing's eyes, seeking to distract it while Tara did the heavy lifting. He lashed out, fueling his power with rage. One of the eyes burst like a balloon full of ink, and the *yokai* screamed.

"Again!" Tara cried.

Craig tried to repeat the trick, but the unfamiliar power was exhausting. He had almost nothing left in the tank. He tried to squeeze another spider eye, and the monster shuddered and writhed. It was producing less silk now, but the two humans were almost immobilized. The monster screeched again and detached itself from the ceiling on a silken rope, descending toward its prey.

"Tara!"

"I know, I know," she moaned.

Two huge limbs swung down toward Craig, and hideously human-looking hands took him by the shoulders and lifted him toward the gaping mouth. Venom-dripping fangs were only a foot or so above Craig's head. He shut his eyes, anticipating his skull being pierced and flooded with toxic filth, but the pain did not come. Instead, the hands gripping him relaxed, and he fell clumsily. He hit his head on something and was dazed for a second. He thought he was seeing stars but realized they were sparks.

Tara had done it.

The spider thing was suddenly frantic with confusion and pain, swinging back and forth. Greasy smoke was coming from its bloated abdomen. Tara had told Craig that she could accelerate the molecules in an object or a living thing. That power wouldn't work on a ghost, which had no material form, but he'd grasped at the straw that this *yokai* was made of something that could heat up. And it seemed he was right.

The monster followed the most basic instinct, retreating upward and then along the ceiling toward the cover of the shadows. But the thing's hair was properly alight now, and it hurtled through the gloom like a grotesque firework, scattering books and boxes as it went. The smoke triggered an alarm, and the sound was even more piercing than the *yokai's* screeching. All they could see of the monster now was a growing blaze in one corner of the room.

Without a word, the duo scrambled to make their way through heaps of flammable material, but the flames were spreading faster, and it was hard to breathe. The open doorway allowed oxygen into the confined space. It was also impossible to tear away all the spiderweb; too much of it had set. Unencumbered, they might have made it, but it seemed that the monster had succeeded. Craig could barely walk or move his arms, and Tara was almost as badly constricted. It would have taken a long minute to remove the debris blocking the door. Now it might take ten or more, and that was time they did not have.

They were going to die in this room.

CHAPTER 25

REUNITED

Coughing, Craig fell to his knees. The smoke had almost blinded him, and his lungs felt full of hot ashes. The alarm was so loud that it was impossible to think. That was why he couldn't make sense of the warm rain that fell suddenly in a cascade on his head, back, and legs. Moments after the rain came a cloud of white snow. That made no sense given the heat.

Seasons in Japan are out of whack, he thought. *They should really do something about it.*

Things got even more confusing when Shane appeared, upside-down and wearing a blue mask over his nose and mouth. That was weird. Craig wondered if Shane was a spider, too, dangling from the ceiling. It seemed unlikely, but a lot of unexpected things had happened lately. Like now, for instance. Craig seemed to be moving along the floor. Shane was dragging him; that was it.

What a nice guy, Craig thought. *Always trying to help.*

They moved out of smoke and darkness into the light. Above Craig now was a pretty Asian girl dressed as a Victorian servant. That was so odd that he wondered if he was dreaming, and then he remembered the café downstairs. The girl knelt by his side and asked if he was okay. She looked a lot less than okay herself. Tearful and scared; traumatized. Craig thought that was so unfair. She'd gone to so much trouble to look nice, and now her makeup was smeared.

"I'm fine," he coughed. "What… where am I?"

She rattled off an address that he didn't catch and then looked up. Craig raised himself on one elbow and saw a half-open door marked 42 with smoke drifting out of the doorway. Shane appeared, carrying Tara over his shoulder. The alarm was still sounding, and Craig wondered how long before the firefighters arrived.

Memory flooded back. They needed to get their gear and leave, fast. Sora's corpse would be found. It would be clear to anyone that the guy hadn't died from smoke inhalation. Craig got up with the café maid's help, and he thanked her. She was still crying.

"The monster... did it kill Sora?" Her eyes pleaded for the answer.

Craig looked down, and muttered a weak, "I'm sorry." She covered her face with her hands and slumped against the wall. Shane held out a mask.

"Come on. Let's get our stuff."

Craig grasped that he was numbed by shock and operating on autopilot. He took the mask and looped the strings around his ears. It helped a little, but his eyes were soon streaming from the smoke. He looked back as he followed Shane into Unit 42. The maid girl had recovered enough to help Tara stand and hobble slowly down the corridor.

Craig trod on something squishy, and a foul stench assaulted his nostrils. He looked down. Even in the dim light, he recognized Sora's clothes, but the man was unrecognizable. The venom of the spider *yokai* had dissolved its victim. Sora was now little more than a patch of dark-brown fluid from which a skull and bones protruded.

"Focus, Craig!"

Shane grabbed the suitcase with the hidden compartment and picked up an air pistol. Craig grabbed a couple of daggers. Then, he saw the bronze mirror and seized it, too.

"What's that?" Shane asked.

"Yelbeghen detector," Craig replied.

They got outside to find the maid girl waiting for them.

"Quick! You need to hide. They're coming."

Craig could already hear the sirens. Being found at the scene of a fire complete with a dissolving corpse would not be good. They followed the girl downstairs, where she ushered them into a store cupboard opposite the café. Seconds later, they heard her talking to the firefighters, who headed upstairs.

"You okay?" Craig asked Tara.

"I've been better," she croaked.

Shane was silent for a few minutes, and when he spoke, he sounded like a man holding in a lot of anger.

"We keep getting blindsided," he said. "We're always losing the initiative. If I hadn't followed you guys, you'd probably be dead. We can't go on like this. We need better intel."

Craig wanted to protest but couldn't fault Shane's reasoning. They hadn't been prepared for Japan. The forces of evil played by different rules. They had made no progress toward finding the Sanagi cult, and they were in no condition for another showdown. Retreat was logical, but he knew Shane wouldn't go for that. Too much might be at stake. Besides, where could they run to? Nowhere in Japan could be deemed safe.

The girl from the café interrupted Craig's thoughts. She led them through into the café, which had been evacuated, and down some back stairs into an alley. They thanked her profusely, and she gave a small bow before vanishing into the crowd. Craig realized they had no idea if she was a Stark operative or just Sora's girlfriend. She had been terrorized into helping the *yokai*, but that upward glance had been a good attempt at a warning. Craig wondered if he would have done any better.

"We smell like smoke," Shane remarked, "but with luck, nobody will bother us."

The usual crowd of onlookers had gathered near the fire truck, but with no smoke or flames emerging, the gawkers were already drifting away. There were quite a few Western tourists around, so it wasn't hard for the three to go with the flow. They were out of sight of the building in minutes. They got a few sidelong glances. They were pretty disheveled, as Craig realized when he saw his reflection in a shop window.

"We can freshen up back at the hotel," Tara said, seeing Craig's expression.

"Yeah," he said resignedly. "Assuming we don't get attacked there again."

They walked on in silence for a while.

"If only there was some way," Craig said, "to stop the cult from tracking us. Some kind of camouflage. Or a psychic cloaking device."

The others were silent. Craig noticed that Tara was flagging a cab. Nobody disagreed and they took a ride back to the hotel. On the way, the car filled with an unpleasant odor. Craig looked at his feet and saw a dark patch on the toe of his right sneaker. Sora was still with them; at least in part. The cabbie said nothing. When Craig paid, he tried to offer a generous tip, but the driver shook his head, and Craig recalled that tipping wasn't part of Japanese culture. The ride had been fairly pricey, anyway.

They trooped into the hotel lobby. Craig was heading straight for the elevators when Shane spoke.

"Eight o'clock; guy sitting there watching us. Looks sketchy."

Craig resisted the temptation to turn around. Instead, he waited by the elevator, his back to what he hoped was eight o'clock. The metal doors offered a blurry reflection of a picture window and a row of seats among potted plants. Only one person sat there. The elevator arrived and disgorged a party of chattering tourists. They stepped aside to let the group pass, and Craig half-turned, pretending to glance around the lobby.

The guy watching them was standing. He was dressed in black and, from his lined face and gray hair, looked to be in his fifties. He was pale and gaunt, but his expression was alert.

"Oh, my God!" Tara squealed.

Craig and Shane stared as she rushed toward the stranger, who smiled and opened his arms.

"What the… is that her Dad?" Shane asked.

"I don't think so." Craig was baffled. "But I guess she knows him."

Tara hugged the pale man tightly, her head on his chest, for a few long moments. Craig felt a sting of jealousy while knowing it was foolish. The guy might not be her father, but he was in that age range. He met the stranger's gaze and had to look away. Something was disturbing in the man's eyes. It was not hostility but still something Craig didn't want to consider. Suffering. Pain. This was a man who had seen too much. It was a look Craig had seen on many ghosts.

"Guys." Tara finally disengaged from the stranger and smiled broadly. "Let me introduce you to an old friend. This is Marcus. Professor Marcus Mortlake."

"The Shadow Trust guy?"

Shane's tone was far from friendly.

"That is correct," Mortlake said. "I assume I'm talking to Shane Ryan?"

"Yeah," Shane said, "but I'm not sure if I want to talk to you."

CHAPTER 26

TRUST ISSUES

Tara started to protest.

"It's all right," Mortlake insisted. "I have a lot of explaining to do. I only hope you'll give me the opportunity."

"I'll hear you out." Shane crossed his arms.

Mortlake looked at Craig and smiled faintly.

"Well, it's nice to finally meet you! I've followed your adventures with interest, believe me. You have an extraordinary talent. Quite unique so far as I can tell."

Craig hesitated, smiling back. He'd heard so much about Mortlake, the Cambridge professor and expert on all things occult. Tara had sought him after a werewolf attack had killed her then-boyfriend. They'd gone on to tackle more paranormal threats in England before Tara had been possessed by a horrendous entity. Mortlake had saved her, but she had returned to the States to put some distance between herself and a terrible trauma.

These and other facts swirled in Craig's head as Mortlake stepped forward and held out a hand. Craig noticed that the man limped slightly. Craig could hardly refuse a handshake, feeling a firm grip and patches of callused flesh. He recalled Tara saying Mortlake had been through a strange ordeal after she'd parted ways with him.

"Nice to meet you, I guess," Craig said.

Mortlake chuckled, and Craig saw laugh lines around his eyes and mouth. The man's eyes, however, showed no hint of humor. Again, Craig wondered how much this man had gone through.

Just because he's suffered doesn't mean you can trust him, he reminded himself.

"Okay," Tara said, "I guess explanations are in order. Why are you here?"

"To help," Mortlake said. "I'm authorized by the Trust to assist you."

Shane gave a skeptical grunt but said nothing. A young Japanese family emerged from the elevators and glanced curiously at the foreigners.

"Guess we should talk somewhere private," Tara said. "But we need to freshen up first. There was a fire."

Mortlake's eyes widened.

"Are you all okay?"

"We're fine," Tara assured him.

Mortlake looked at Shane.

"I would suggest talking in a quiet café or somewhere like that. But there's something I need to show you all, and it can't be revealed in public."

Shane raised an eyebrow but remained silent. Then he turned and pressed the elevator button. The doors opened immediately.

"Guess you'd better come up," Tara said.

Half an hour later, Craig emerged from the bathroom in fresh clothes to find Tara and Mortlake chatting happily over cups of tea. He felt sure now that they were old friends, and that the English professor was a kind of favorite uncle to her or a trusted mentor.

"Protection is what I can offer you," Mortlake said, "to some extent. No shield is flawless, of course. With a lot of help, I think I have something of value, but I need to talk to all three of you together. In the meantime, perhaps you could bring me up to speed about your mission so far?"

Twenty minutes later, Mortlake set down his teacup.

"You've had quite an adventure," he said. "Twenty-four hours of excitement. And now you share each other's talents; that's almost unheard of. Your ghost samurai and the *kami* of the shrine presumably want to keep Yelbeghen at bay. The ordeal was quite an elaborate way to empower you all, I agree. But most such rituals are not dramatic."

Mortlake asked to see the bronze mirror. He confessed to knowing nothing about it and failed to get the image of Yelbeghen to move.

"Guess that's good news." Craig took back the mirror and secreted it in the trick suitcase.

Mortlake peered into the false compartment. Shane entered as he was checking their weapons. Standing by the door, he studied the newcomer, his expression neutral.

"I can provide you with more equipment," Mortlake said. "The usual—tasers, et cetera. I also have radios and satellite phones, which are essential for effective teamwork outside cell service range."

Mortlake paused, looking at Shane, but if the latter was impressed, he didn't show it. The Englishman continued.

"As I said, there's also a special defense tailored to this country's unique dangers."

Shane gave a slight snort.

"All I see is a British guy who's been through the wringer. Okay, you get points for surviving this far, and from what I've heard you're smart and tough. But you're gonna have to do more than talk a good game. What's this miracle defense against the *yokai*?"

Mortlake didn't reply. Instead, he took off his jacket and placed it on the back of a chair.

"Would you mind closing the curtains?" he asked Craig.

Craig obliged as the Englishman unbuttoned his shirt. Shane saw pale skin exposed in the gloom. Mortlake reached for his jacket and took out a small object, offering it to Shane.

"Blacklight," Mortlake said. "Please; it's quicker if you just see it."

Shane took the flashlight.

"This had better be good," he grumbled.

The strange glow of ultraviolet illuminated the half-naked man. Craig stared. He had not known what to expect. He could never have predicted what was revealed.

"Oh, my God!" Tara gasped.

Where the ultraviolet light played on Mortlake's torso, bright indigo markings appeared. Japanese characters covered almost every inch of exposed skin. Mortlake turned slowly, his arms raised, to show that his entire upper body was covered with writing. Craig felt frustrated that he could not read Japanese: Shane's power only extended to spoken language.

"What are they?" he blurted out.

"Extracts from sacred writings," Mortlake explained, "along with spells, incantations, and a few straightforward threats to evil spirits. They were devised and applied by local experts."

"And they work?" Shane asked.

"They have worked for centuries," Mortlake replied, "but nothing is one hundred percent effective. Their main power is to make it hard for paranormal entities to see you. Also, they render you unpleasant or even painful to their touch. With this protection, the Sanagi cult will no longer be able to track you, at least not by occult means. They could, of course, still use conventional techniques."

"Huh."

Shane stepped closer, examining the elaborate markings. Then, he switched off the flashlight.

"Okay," he said, "you've got my interest. The people who apply this stuff are here in Tokyo?"

"I can take you to them right away," Mortlake assured him, putting his shirt back on. "They're at a Buddhist temple in the Edogawa district."

"Not so fast," Shane said firmly. "I want to know just how the Shadow Trust is involved in all this."

Mortlake sighed.

"That is a long story, but you are entitled to it. Best be sitting comfortably. Then, I'll begin."

He took another sip of tea and then set the cup down.

"The Shadow Trust exists to keep things stable within fairly roomy limits. They don't want death and destruction on a grand scale. The organization was set up to gather information on the occult and mysterious, then moved on to exploiting paranormal powers and entities. But all to one end. Stability, which is probably the most difficult thing anyone can aspire to."

Mortlake was so professorial that Craig had to resist the temptation to raise his hand. He cleared his throat instead, and the Englishman paused.

"Um, okay, but we've heard the Trust can't be—you know—trusted? I mean, okay, I know you guys kind of helped us in Scotland. But how do we know you don't want this idol for yourselves?"

Mortlake shook his head firmly.

"The idol of Yelbeghen should be destroyed if possible. If not, sunk into the ocean depths. Nobody should control it. The Trust helped you in Scotland because the mercenaries trying to kill you were the greater evil. And I'm here now because I want to help, but I do have an ulterior motive. A personal one."

Mortlake hesitated and looked down at his hands, folded in his lap.

"Is it Lynn?" Tara asked quietly.

"Yes." The Englishman looked up at Shane. "If I neutralize Yelbeghen, someone I care about very much will be freed from a terrible captivity. Demonic possession."

For the first time, Craig saw the surprise on Shane's face. Surprise, and perhaps a trace of compassion. Shane rubbed his chin, looking Mortlake in the eye.

"Two good motives for the price of one, eh? Well, I guess we're allies of convenience—for the time being, anyhow. But I still want to see this special camo of yours in action."

Mortlake stood and gestured to the door.

"Let's go out now and confuse some Tokyo ghosts."

It wasn't difficult to find a ghost. They looked out for a dead man in a suit who seemed lost. A salaryman caught between his loyalty to his company and his household. Shane was first to spot one, on the corner near their hotel. Mortlake gave a curt nod and approached the ghost, weaving through the crowd.

The other three moved closer to spectate, forming a small circle around which living pedestrians flowed. At first, it seemed as if the spirit would not react to the Englishman. The ghost continued to stand and stare mournfully at nothing. But then, as Mortlake got within a yard or so, the expression on the specter's face changed. There was puzzlement, followed by a wrinkling of the nose, and a frown of distaste. The ghost looked around, seeking the new, unpleasant factor in its long postmortem existence.

"The ghost can't see him." Shane was surprised. "That is pretty neat. Of course, this is kind of a feeble ghost. But still, not bad."

Mortlake waited until the flow of foot traffic eased a little, giving him a clear line to the ghost. Then, he reached out a hand and gently touched the ghost on the shoulder. The ghost flinched and took a step backward. It collided with a young masked woman who was staring at her phone. She looked up, her eyes wide, and gave Mortlake a hard look, but he was too far away to have touched her. She scurried away with her head down.

The ghost spent a few seconds looking around and then returned to simply standing and staring at nothing. Mortlake, again choosing his moment, lunged forward and flung his arms around the ghost. A few passersby looked at him, then hurried on. The ghost flailed his arms, its mouth wide with surprise and fear, and vanished.

"No doubt he'll be back," Mortlake remarked as he rejoined the group. "But as you see, the characters are quite effective. And the dye will last a good few months before fading."

"Okay, I'm sold," Shane said.

CHAPTER 27

THE NAKED AND THE DEAD

Mortlake took them by cab to a Buddhist temple in the Edogawa district. In contrast to last night's shrine, the temple lay just off a main street. Its entrance was flanked by stone lions that looked more cheerful than ferocious. They were greeted on the threshold by a shaven-headed monk in a saffron robe who surprised Craig by speaking good English. Seeing this reaction, the monk smiled benignly.

"I studied business management at UCLA but got kind of bored with the family business. It involved working with raw fish every day, and eventually, I felt the fish were judging me. Those eyes. So, I decided to do a little meditating and learn another kind of truth."

Mortlake said he would wait at the entrance, as he had no particular desire to see any of them naked. The monk led them through the temple past worshippers kneeling before a ten-foot-tall statue of the Buddha. Incense and the sound of prayer gave the shadowy space a timeless feel. Craig's spirits rose. Tara trusted Mortlake, so he was inclined to do the same. And getting the experts on your side was surely sensible.

The monk led them behind a curtain and opened a door. They crossed a small courtyard and then entered a low building where two more shaven-headed people knelt. At first, Craig thought the two were a man and a boy, but he realized he was looking at a Buddhist nun. A small brazier was burning in one corner. On a tripod stand, a clay jar bubbled. The nun rose and smiled at Tara, gesturing to a corner of the room. A painted screen stood against the wall, waiting to be unfolded.

"The sister will take care of you," the lead monk said.

"Time to shed my inhibitions, I guess." Tara grinned at the others.

After she'd been led away, Craig and Shane stripped off their clothing and seated themselves on low stools. They had their backs to one another by a kind of unspoken agreement. The lead monk dealt with Craig while his subordinate painted Shane.

"Do you do this a lot?" Craig wondered aloud.

"Mortlake-san was my first customer in many years," the monk replied, dipping a brush into a small bowl of tea-colored liquid. "It was an interesting challenge."

Craig looked up at the monk's unwrinkled face and clear eyes.

"Many years? You don't seem that old."

The monk smiled.

"Time is a difficult concept for the wise, and a simple one for the thoughtless."

Craig was unsure whether he'd been insulted or praised, so decided to shut up for a while. Then, a thought struck him.

"This isn't going to hurt, is it?"

"It might sting a bit," the monk admitted and began to write on Craig's left shoulder.

The paint stung, but not too badly at first. The problem was that, as more of his body was covered with characters and symbols, the cumulative effect of the dye became troubling. It wasn't just physical discomfort: Waves of nausea and dizziness coursed through Craig's body. Weird colored trails and halos enveloped the monk as he moved, and the light from the windows became harsh.

"Close your eyes, please," the monk said.

"You're going to paint my eyelids?"

There was no response, just another patient smile. Craig did as he was asked. The brush dabbed at his flesh and exerted pressure on one eyeball, then another. A few moments later, Craig saw bizarre, phosphorescent patterns swirling across his field of vision. He wondered, belatedly, if the paint contained hallucinogens that could be absorbed through the skin.

"You can open them now." The monk moved on to his ears.

The light in the room was almost unbearably bright now. Craig felt like he would throw up, even though he hadn't eaten for hours. He also had a throbbing headache. Combined with the general nausea, the result was very much like a bad hangover.

"Does everyone feel bad when you do this?" he asked.

The monk, who had been working on Craig's back, paused.

"There should only be slight discomfort. What is wrong?"

Craig described the symptoms. The monk looked at Craig's face and felt his pulse. For the first time, the hairless man looked puzzled. Then, an idea struck him.

"You are the one who moves on the souls of the dead?"

Craig admitted that he was.

"I see."

The monk leaned closer, peering into Craig's eyes.

"How many have you moved on in this way?"

Craig blinked in confusion.

"In my life? God, I don't know. Maybe a hundred? A little more, perhaps. Not more than one-fifty."

The monk's eyes widened.

"I never thought there were so many," he said. "And each one leaving a part of itself, a fingerprint on your soul. You are troubled because all those you helped are still with you, albeit to a tiny degree."

Craig started to slump sideways, and the monk caught him before he could fall off the stool.

"I can't be possessed," Craig protested. "That's not how it works. I moved them on!"

The monk shook his head, laying down his brush so he could support Craig with both hands.

"The spirits of the dead are tormented by the sacred writings. Your body is haunted by the dead, those you thought gone forever. Nothing is ever truly created or destroyed. All things linger, albeit unseen. They have become part of you, Craig. I will proceed more slowly now. And let me find you something to ease the discomfort."

He led Craig to a bench where he could be propped up more easily and then left the room after speaking to his assistants. Fascinated despite his condition, Craig watched Shane being slowly covered with a layer of mystical protection. The brownish characters remained visible for a few minutes, fading slowly until they became invisible. It was a neat trick, allowing the monk to be sure they'd gotten the brush strokes correct before his handiwork vanished.

The head monk returned with a steaming cup of jasmine tea. Craig took a sip, found it pleasant, and swallowed a mouthful, then half-drained the cup.

"Wait for a minute or so," the monk advised. "The effect should be apparent then."

Craig waited as his headache diminished. The light seemed less harsh, and the sensation of nausea receded. He finished the tea and thanked the monk. The latter resumed painting Craig's body, but taking his time. Tara emerged from behind her screen with the nun just as Shane was getting dressed. Explanations followed.

"So," Tara looked Craig up and down, "does this mean the traces of the ghosts he's moved on will disappear?"

"It is unlikely," the head monk said. "They are part of him. The earliest are as real and vital as any memory. You might call them spiritual memories as much as fingerprints. Or, if you like, echoes of souls. There are many ways to look at the matter."

Shane grunted and said he'd wait outside. Craig watched him go.

"You think he wanted to spare me further embarrassment?" he asked Tara.

She smiled at the thought.

"I doubt it. He's not one for social niceties. Probably just his Marine training—don't get shut inside a small building with only one exit."

Craig tried hard not to think about what Tara had seen, or what she might think of him. It wasn't as if he could make a joke about cold weather. He noticed that the nun had left, which was something. The discomfort from the ink made him itchy, so it was hard to keep still. But, perhaps thanks to his surroundings, he found some inner serenity and didn't do anything to smear the monk's handiwork.

"All done."

The bald man sat back on his haunches, and Craig looked down to see the last traces of ink fading into his feet and ankles.

"I don't feel protected," he said half-seriously.

"Then try harder," the monk said. "Believing helps."

CHAPTER 28
REACHING KYOTO

"Stop wriggling," Tara said in a stage whisper. "We all have to tough it out."

"Sorry; I'm just getting comfortable," Craig replied.

He glanced around the train car. Nobody was looking. But then, half the seats were empty, and the Japanese were so reserved that it was hard to be sure how many of the passengers were ghosts. Nobody had noticed Craig shifting in his seat.

Craig had spent two hours the previous day stark naked and being painted with invisible ink by a monk. Mortlake had not mentioned one side effect of his ghostly defense system: It tingled and itched. The Englishman had assured him the irritation would wear off after a few hours, but it had kept Craig up for most of the night. He had half-hoped for a ghostly incursion to test their new defenses, but nothing had materialized.

Now Craig, Tara, and Mortlake were on the *Shinkansen*, a high-speed train, heading south to Kyoto. Shane had elected to stay behind in Tokyo for now. Craig had suspected that Shane wanted to try out his new camouflage unhampered by their motley gang. In the end, a lone wolf could only be a team player for so long.

"So, Professor Tanaka." Craig twisted around in his seat to talk to Mortlake. "He's one of yours?"

"Not exactly," Mortlake replied. "His son was a low-ranking Shadow Trust operative. Really just assigned to gather information on the Sanagi cult. It seems he got too close to the truth and was killed. The professor is an expert on folklore and obscure beliefs. He knows a lot about the cult, but whether he will share is debatable. I don't think he approved of his son's involvement with shady foreigners like me."

Craig mulled over that information as the bullet train headed south. The discomfort from the ink on his skin was slowly fading. He dozed eventually but was awakened by Tara after an hour or so. They had arrived in Kyoto, the ancient capital of Japan and a center of traditional scholarship. Soon, they were vying with ordinary tourists for one of the scarce cabs. The heat and humidity were oppressive, hitting them all the harder as they'd enjoyed good air conditioning on the train.

While they waited and perspired, Craig tried to pick out the local ghosts. It wasn't as easy as it was in Tokyo. A sizeable number of locals and tourists were dressed in traditional costume, either the full kimono or the simplified version called the *yukata*. The result was an ever-shifting vista of people in bright garments popping up amid the multitudes in drabber Western clothes. Distinguishing the living from the dead proved almost impossible unless someone walked through a ghost.

Just when he was growing bored with the game, Craig spotted a woman approaching in a very elaborate costume. From her ornate hairdo to her built-up sandals, she looked the picture of an old-time *geisha*. She approached, taking swift, tiny steps, her eyes downcast, and her hair ornaments glistening in the noonday sun. Craig had resolved to reach out and startle her when he noticed people around him aiming their phones. He had been planning to assault a woman.

"A remarkable tradition," Mortlake said, following his gaze.

"I thought she was a ghost," Craig admitted.

"Time makes ghosts of us all, I suppose," Mortlake said quietly. "One way or another."

It was an odd thing to say, and it confirmed Craig's view of the Englishman as a troubled man, someone who could never rest easy. He recalled Tara telling him about Mortlake's kindness, sense of humor, and intellect. But whenever Craig talked to the man, he got a sense of all-embracing sadness.

It's like he's in mourning for himself, Craig thought.

They finally got a taxi. The address Mortlake had for Professor Tanaka proved to be in a pleasant suburb on the outskirts of Kyoto. Tanaka had agreed to a meeting, but when the academic opened the door, his expression was far from welcoming. After they'd swapped their outdoor shoes for slippers, Tanaka showed them into a traditional Japanese living room where a woman in a dark blue kimono waited. There was a teapot and cups on a low table.

"Please, sit," Tanaka said.

The professor was a short, broad-shouldered man with an untidy mass of iron-gray hair. He wore glasses with thick tortoiseshell frames. Craig suspected that he took no nonsense from his students. Mrs. Tanaka, by contrast, was a graceful fortysomething woman with a sad, kindly expression. Craig accepted some tea and thanked his hostess. She looked slightly surprised at his command of the language and asked how he had learned it.

"Oh," he said, flustered, "I watch a lot of anime."

Mortlake, whose Japanese was almost nonexistent, asked Tara to translate for him. He began by expressing condolences for the death of their son, a sentiment the Americans echoed. The professor gave a curt, formal acknowledgment. His wife bowed but said nothing. Craig got the impression she was holding back her emotions as etiquette required.

"My son," Tanaka went on, "forged links with the Shadow Trust despite my misgivings. He saw himself as a champion of good against evil. Nothing wrong with that, of course, but he was in over his head. Officially, of course, he died from hypothermia after his car was immobilized. Do you, Mortlake-san, have any further information on that topic?"

The Englishman looked surprised.

"I'm afraid I don't know any more than you," he said and then waited for Tara to translate.

Tanaka looked disappointed but said nothing more. The professor's wife stood and stammered out an apology before hurrying out of the room.

"Please forgive her," Tanaka said. "She has been very concerned about our son's soul. She is afraid that, because he died an unnatural death, he cannot pass on. She prays a great deal. It brings some consolation."

Mortlake and Tara tried to move the conversation back to the cult. Craig, feeling superfluous, looked around the room. Mrs. Tanaka had left a sliding door slightly open as she left, and a gap of about six inches showed the room next door. It held what Craig realized was a kind of altar. Incense burned in front of a photograph. It was hard to make out from a distance, but Craig could guess who was in the picture.

Someone moved in the other room, blocking Craig's view of the shrine. At first, he thought it was Mrs. Tanaka, but then he saw the figure was far larger. Through the narrow gap, Craig saw little of the newcomer, except that he wore heavy clothes unsuited for the stifling late-summer weather. The figure moved out of sight, but not before Craig saw a patch of white on one shoulder of his coat. Craig stood, stopping the conversation.

"Professor, did the police return your son's possessions after his death?"

"Yes, of course," Tanaka said. "Why do you ask?"

Craig explained as best he could. Some object—perhaps a gift from a loved one—could anchor a soul to this world. Before he finished, Tanaka had jumped up and gone to the sliding door. He opened it to reveal a young man in winter clothes, staring at the altar on which his photograph rested. Tanaka's wife reappeared then, her eyes and nose slightly reddened. Craig repeated what he'd told her husband, adding that he had helped many spirits leave the earthly realm.

"You can send my Yuta to the Pure Land?" she breathed.

"I will do my best," Craig said.

When he'd asked Mortlake if the writing on his skin would interfere with his main power, the answer had been a definite maybe. That hadn't satisfied Craig, so he had asked the Buddhist monk who painted his body for some help. They had come through, albeit in a rather daunting way.

"I'm with you, Craig," Tara said.

The ghost reacted to the presence of the living for the first time, turning to look at his parents. Tanaka's face was blue-white with cold, and his lips were so dark, they seemed black by contrast. Beneath his eyes lay a delicate trace of frozen tears. Craig stepped forward and spoke.

"I am here to help."

The ghost's eyes flicked back and forth to locate the speaker. Craig remained invisible to the ghost, proof of the effectiveness of the mystical characters. Now came the hard part. Craig continued, explaining that he could help Yuta reach the Pure Land. The ghost seemed unsure, still baffled as to why he couldn't see Craig. Explanations followed. Yuta remained doubtful.

"Marcus Mortlake is here," Tara added. "He thanks you for your courage and dedication."

"I would like to see him—see *any* of you!" the ghost said.

Mortlake stepped into the room.

"If you come closer, toward the doorway, you will see me more clearly. It may be unpleasant, but if you persist, I think you will recognize me."

Yuta walked forward. Craig saw the ghost's expression change from puzzlement to distress. He flinched and stepped away. The critical distance from Mortlake was about eighteen inches.

"You saw him?" Craig asked. "You know it's Mortlake?"

Yuta nodded, his expression now determined and almost fanatical.

"I acknowledge my *senpai* and wish to report my findings!"

CHAPTER 29

DEBRIEFING AND DECISION

"That's what I call work ethic," Craig said quietly. "Guy's gonna put in that report, and being dead won't stop him."

Yuta's debriefing took a while, what with the need for Tara to relay the information and translate for the parents as their son spoke to Mortlake in English. The story was a relatively simple one. After online discussions with Mortlake and other Trust operatives, Yuta had agreed to seek out the cult. Tracking down leads had proved difficult, but thanks to his father's scholarship, Yuta had gotten a lead. This had taken him north to the prefecture of Aomori.

"Unfortunately, it was winter by the time he got a precise location," Tara explained.

Craig looked at the snow and ice that burdened the ghost and shuddered. Yuta spoke again.

"The place the cult had sought refuge was called Yomimura. The village of the dead."

Seek the village of the dead, Craig thought. *Those were Shiro's last words.*

As Yuta continued his tale, Craig noticed that Tara was careful to play down some of the grimmer details to the Tanakas. But she could not hide the raw facts. Car trouble had led Yuta to seek refuge in an abandoned building. There, he had fallen victim to one of the deadliest *yokai,* the Woman of the Snow.

"Fascinating," Mortlake said. "A kind of vampire unique to Japan. I had wondered if she was real or a garbled account of a particularly lethal ghost."

Craig noticed that, as Yuta spoke of his death, the room became appreciably cooler. What was more, flakes of snow swirled around the ghost in a nonexistent breeze, glinting in a slanting shaft of sunlight. It was a beautiful effect, so fascinating that for a moment, Craig forgot that these were memories of a terrible death made manifest.

Yuta went on to explain that, as Mortlake had suspected, his unquiet spirit had been attached to the watch given him as a graduation gift by his mother. When she heard this, Mrs. Tanaka seemed about to break down again. Her husband put an arm around her and spoke gently, doing his best to console her.

"We can help him," Craig reiterated. "Yuta, come as close to me as you can."

The ghost approached, but as he got within a couple of feet of Craig, Yuta's face registered revulsion. Craig tried to reach out with his mind but found himself unable to focus. Yuta's presence was blurred and distorted. It was as he'd feared: The mystical barrier that protected him against supernatural attacks worked both ways. It was like a paranormal smokescreen.

"I can't reach him," Tara whispered. "You got anything?"

"No," Craig replied. "No, damn it."

Yuta staggered backward. He was a tragic figure, surrounded by swirling flakes of snow that faded in and out of sight. He was glad the guy's parents couldn't see their son. He smiled at the Tanakas and explained that he had to perform a ritual before he could continue.

"It is," he added, "a cleansing of a sort."

Mortlake and Tara looked concerned. The Englishman reached out and touched Craig lightly on the arm.

"Are you sure? If you do this, you'll be laying yourself open—"

"I know," Craig said tersely. "But I said I'd help him, and I will."

He retrieved his bag from the hallway and took out a small clay jar sealed with red wax.

"May I use your bathroom?" he asked Yuta's father.

"Of course." The professor was puzzled but indicated a door opposite the shrine room.

Craig went into the bathroom, closed the door, and looked at himself in the mirror above the sink. He saw a man with a not-unpleasant face, eyes that some called kind, and a jaw that was maybe a little weak. He thought of Yuta Tanaka, of a mother's torment, and a father's stoical despair.

He took off his shirt and then fumbled with the clay jar's seal. When he finally opened it, he almost spilled the contents. It was a thin, pale, yellow liquid with a faint, floral odor. He tipped some into his palm and then rubbed it over his chest. The slight tingling from the protective markings grew suddenly more intense before dwindling to nothing but a slight numbness. He repeated the process until he had rubbed the tincture over his torso, arms, and face.

With luck, that would be enough.

He was about to rejoin the others when he remembered something. He reached into the back pocket of his jeans and found a dark red velvet drawstring bag. It was the *onimori* he'd been given by Sora a minute or so before the man had been killed. A talisman against evil. It seemed like a feeble thing now, something that might be sold to tourists.

"Still, better safe than sorry," Craig murmured.

He looped the string around his neck and tucked the bag down his shirt front. Craig emerged from the bathroom and returned to the shrine room, where the Tanakas—all three of them—were waiting. Yuta was looking longingly at his mother, who was gazing right through him at his graduation photo. Craig walked closer until he was standing just more than a foot away from Yuta, who did not react. That was promising.

"I think I can do this now," he told Tara.

Mortlake muttered something under his breath. Tara gave a thumbs-up sign. Yuta turned to face Craig, standing stiffly as if he were facing a firing squad. Craig chose his words carefully, as he could hardly ask the guy if he felt comfortable.

"You feel no discomfort in my presence?"

"No," Yuta responded.

"You wish to venture to the Pure Land?"

"Yes."

Craig closed his eyes and repeated a silent mantra to clear his mind of extraneous thoughts. He could sense Yuta's spirit and no longer felt any interference. His confidence returned, and he reached out again. The power he had gained at Grendon Mill surged through him, no longer dammed up by the mystical barrier. He coaxed Yuta's troubled spirit to soar, to find its way to an afterlife.

Suddenly, Craig was looking out at a wintry landscape. Cold wrapped him in a cruel embrace, and the hot Kyoto climate was banished. He was in a nondescript room. It was night. Outside, the sky blazed with an aurora. The light in the heavens formed a seven-headed monster, rearing up over the world. Then, his viewpoint shifted. A woman knelt beside him, her face pale and beautiful. She leaned closer and spoke the last words Yuta heard as a living man.

The kiss of the snow vampire pierced Craig like an icicle through the heart, but the agony was fleeting. Craig opened his eyes to see the familiar ragged whirlpool of light above the ghost's head. As the vortex widened, it revealed a seascape. A *torii* stood, half-submerged, off a rocky coast. As the vista grew broader, Craig saw a beach, a small bungalow, and a group of children playing in the sand. In the middle distance, some people were flying a kite. A mundane scene, yet everything was bathed in an unearthly golden light. It was a paradise built of summer memories, a world of innocence and beauty all the better for its grounding in the commonplace.

"Yes," Craig breathed. "It is the Pure Land. It is waiting for you. All your friends. All those happy days."

Yuta's ghost began to rise toward the portal as Craig held it open almost without effort. The power coursing through him had never seemed stronger. It was a wonderful thing to move a soul on to a better world. The snowflakes that had circled Yuta twinkled out of existence as sunlight melted the dusting of snow on his clothes. His tears unfroze, flowed briefly, and vanished. All traces of the Snow Woman's deadly kiss were gone, and a smiling Yuta vanished into the vortex.

Wonderful, Craig thought. *So perfect. So beautiful.*

He stared up at the portal, which was now changing from one mesmerizing color to another. Yuta's Pure Land was gone, replaced by a scene that was familiar but elusive. A river valley. Mountains. Smoke arising from a small cabin on a riverbend. Here again were peace and harmony illuminated by the same golden light. Craig wanted to reach up through the portal and touch that perfect world. It was absurd of course, but he knew it was possible. And it would only take a moment…

"Hey!"

Someone was slapping his cheek, and not very gently. Tara was looking down at him with wide, anxious eyes. Craig realized he was lying on the floor of the living room. Mortlake was kneeling on his other side, holding his wrist.

"You seem to have fainted. Your pulse is normal, though. Whatever happened doesn't seem to have been too shocking. Probably just overexertion in this hot weather."

They helped him to his feet. The Tanakas looked on, anxiety written on their faces but too polite to demand answers.

"I'm sorry to have alarmed you," he told them. "It went well, despite my little accident. Your son is no longer troubled. He has left this world."

The Tanakas broke down. Craig sensed that the professor had held in his grief for too long. Now, it was the wife's turn to comfort her husband. Mortlake glanced at the door, and the others took the cue. They thanked the couple for their hospitality and left.

"The village of the dead," Mortlake said as they emerged into the punishing heat. "In Aomori prefecture. That's quite a journey. I'd feel more confident if your friend Mr. Ryan was with us."

Tara didn't respond. Instead, she asked Craig what he planned to do about his occult camouflage.

"Guess I'll be invisible from the waist down." He smiled. "Kind of like my love life, right?"

Tara didn't find that funny.

"Just to be clear, we know ghosts can't kill you, but we're not sure about paranormal entities. What if they can? You're taking a hell of a risk. Please, think again!"

Craig tried to take her hand, but she pulled away. He looked over at Mortlake, who was eyeing him speculatively.

"Do you agree with her, Marcus?"

"It seems to me," the Englishman said, "that you're taking a serious risk, albeit a calculated one. I'm not sure who's right, but the power to move on troubled souls is no trivial thing. And we can be sure word is spreading that a very special seer is in Japan."

Craig thought about that for a while. Sometimes, he concluded, there was such a thing as bad publicity.

CHAPTER 30

THE IMAGE OF THE BEAST

"Still nothing?" Tara asked.

Craig made a negative noise. It was difficult to project the image from the bronze mirror. The serpent wobbled and blurred. Now and again, he managed to hold it steady for a few seconds. The seven-headed monster moved for a moment, but so little, it might have been illusory.

"Guess we're not getting closer. At least not yet."

Tara clucked her tongue.

"Assuming that thing works as advertised. Magic gizmos are tricky."

Craig put the mirror into his bag and leaned back in his seat as the landscape hurtled by outside. They were on the bullet train north to Aomori, the northernmost city on the main island of Honshu.

They'd briefly talked to Shane after leaving the Tanakas' and he'd said he was still following his leads. The newly formed threesome was keen to act on the information it had received from Yuta Tanaka's ghost.

The plan was to find Yomimura in the foothills south of Aomori. A little research had shown that the village had been a leper colony in feudal Japan, a place of banishment. Then, a plague had struck it, and the population never recovered. Yomimura was abandoned sometime in the sixties. Sometime after that, the Sanagi cult had made it their base.

"Does our friend Crutchley have anything to say about it?" Craig nodded at the book on Tara's lap.

"Nah, not as far as I can see," she admitted. "I had high hopes for the guy, but almost the whole book is about the apocalypse. He seemed to get a big kick out of it."

"Can I take a look?"

"Be my guest."

She handed the battered book of prophecy to Craig, and he carefully turned the yellowed pages. The small, faded print coupled with the old-fashioned English made for a difficult read. A passage leaped out at him now and again, but only because it seemed bizarre or downright twisted. Flipping through the book felt increasingly like studying a madman's diary. The overall tone was set by passages like, "The faithless will have their entrails wound upon a cylinder of brass," and, "The eyes of the corrupt will be plucked out by carrion hawks."

Then Craig came to, "Great cities will be shaken into ruins amid fire and lamentation." He reread that last sentence. When they arrived in Japan, they'd been asked to download disaster warning apps. A lot of government information had been provided about what to do if a megaquake hit. Crutchley was probably drawing on Biblical passages for his ideas, but it was still slightly unnerving. Craig read around the bit about fire and lamentation and discovered a reference to "the sacred mountain" raining fire and brimstone on the faithful. He recalled that Mount Fuji was classified as an active volcano.

"Interesting," Tara admitted when he pointed these facts out. "You have a good eye for that stuff. I guess I got bogged down in his denouncing whoremongers and moneychangers and stuff."

Mortlake, who was sitting behind them, leaned forward between the seats.

"Can I take a look? I've heard of Crutchley but never seen a copy. Even the Trust doesn't have one."

Craig handed the book to him. He then looked out at the fields and small villages as they raced by and thought of Yelbeghen, a monster of immense power reborn in Japan, the nation with more natural disasters per square mile than any other. He recalled a map showing the Ring of Fire, a chain of fault lines in the earth's crust that passed through Japan and extended around most of the Pacific Ocean. Craig thought of Sanagi and how much the fanatic had hated the modern world. What if his cult gained the power to destroy much of that world or perhaps dislocate it economically and politically so that civilization plunged into a death spiral?

Craig outlined his thoughts to the others. Tara, from a scientist's perspective, said that vast amounts of energy would be needed to trigger a major seismic event. Mortlake agreed.

"But," he added, "we have no idea how powerful Yelbeghen might have been, and what it might become. A being that has lain dormant for centuries, perhaps millennia, could be relatively weak when awoken. Or it could have recharged its batteries and become unimaginably powerful. The point is that we don't know. All we can do is try to destroy the idol or—if that's impossible—put it out of reach. Well, human reach."

"Wouldn't destroying it be easy?" Craig asked. "I mean, the legend is that the idol was smashed up, right? All seven heads were broken off. So, you could just smash what's left with a hammer, right?"

Mortlake sounded amused.

"The direct approach. I like it. I hope we get the chance."

The Englishman sat back and resumed his perusal of the book of prophecy, and Craig went back to daydreaming and dozing. The bullet train pulled into the big city of Sendai. As they drew into the station, Craig saw a statue of the city's mascot, a kind of anime samurai figure. Every city and company in Japan had a mascot of some kind. They were modern versions of the *kami*, he thought, only cuter and easier to put on a T-shirt or keyring.

After they left Sendai, the tracks curved slightly and offered Craig another chance to experiment with the bronze mirror. Again, he struggled to keep the disk steady. Finally, he projected an image onto the back of the seat in front of him. The seven-headed creature appeared as a static image. That was vaguely disappointing. If the idol was in the north, shouldn't there be a sign?

"No service, huh?" Tara leaned forward to peer at the circle of light.

Then, it happened. The image of the beast faded and was replaced by a bizarre montage of flickering shapes. Craig realized he was looking at human faces that changed rapidly as they blurred into one another. The effect was fleeting, and the now-familiar shape of Yelbeghen returned in a second or so. Then, the sunlight faded. Craig looked out the train window to see a raft of dark clouds covering the western sky.

"What the hell was that?" Tara asked.

"Faces," Craig said. "I think—did you recognize anyone?"

She looked troubled and glanced back to where Mortlake was absorbed in Crutchley's book.

"I think I saw Marcus, but it's hard to be sure. It was just for a second."

Craig stared at her, confused.

"I didn't recognize Marcus," he admitted, "but I think I saw your face."

They looked at the mirror, which lay on Craig's lap.

"It's messing with us," Tara said. "Magical items do that. Screw with your mind."

She turned to speak to Mortlake, who was intrigued.

"The Trust knows about these kinds of mirrors," he explained, "but this particular one must have slipped under their radar. Tara's right, Craig. Any magical artifact of unknown provenance could be deceitful, even if this Sora chap gave it to you in good faith. Pity we can't ask him where he got it."

Craig thought of his last sight of Sora's disfigured corpse and felt suddenly cold. Something else troubled him; something that he'd almost forgotten. He almost had it for a moment but forgot it again. Now, it would bug him for hours, and it was probably trivial, anyway.

Tara and Mortlake talked some more while the train hurtled northwest toward Aomori. The sun showed no sign of emerging from the clouds.

Craig suggested using a flashlight to project an image, remembering that Sora had used artificial light to demonstrate the mirror's strange power.

"Why not?"

Mortlake rummaged in his bag and produced a powerful flashlight. Craig did his best to project an image onto the seatback. The reflection of the monster moved briefly, its snakelike necks waving, and then froze again. There was no further hint of movement or flashes of familiar faces. Craig tried for a few minutes, but he only succeeded in earning a disapproving look from a passing woman. If it hadn't been for Tara seeing something odd as well, Craig might have suspected a simple hallucination.

"A pity," Mortlake said. "As I said, though, magical artifacts are notoriously tricky."

"You think this thing has some kind of soul trapped in it?" Craig held up the mirror and turned it around. "Like the McIvor sword?"

"Possibly," Mortlake said. "Sometimes, magicians used the soul of a hapless victim as a kind of spiritual power source. It's like the practice of sacrificing children and burying them in the foundations of bridges and other structures. Horrible, of course, but very effective. And there's Simon Magus in the Acts of the Apostles … but I'm not here to deliver a lecture."

"Thank heaven for small mercies," Tara observed.

Craig put away the *makyo*, wondering what this new development signified. It seemed that they were making some progress. Once more, the combined effects of sleeplessness and jet lag caught up with him, and he dozed. When he next checked the view from the window, the landscape had changed. They were racing through a mountain pass flanked by impressive forests. The trees were conifers, mantling the lower slopes in deep green.

"Are we in Aomori yet?" he asked.

"Yep." Tara held up her phone. "Mr. Google says we crossed the border a few minutes ago. Want something to eat?"

There was no food for sale on the train, so they had bought some snacks at the station.

"Yeah, why not?"

Tara opened a shopping bag and laid out wrapped sandwiches, bags of chips, candy bars, and cans of soda. There was also *onigiri*, a kind of rice ball with a tuna filling. Craig opted for an egg sandwich, chips, and a rice ball. All but one of the cans contained Coke, which he wasn't in the mood for. He and Tara reached for the solitary lemon soda at the same time.

"Okay, you take it," he said, smiling.

"Flip you for it," she said. "Heads or tails?"

Craig looked at the copper coin poised on her thumbnail. It caught a stray ray of sunlight from the window, making the tiny image of Japan's emperor shine brightly.

"Heads or tails?" she repeated. "Earth to Craig! Come in, please?"

He shook his head and laughed.

"Sorry, but… 'heads must be taken!' Why did it say that?"

CHAPTER 31

TALKING HEADS, COUNTING CASH

The three discussed Craig's question as the train sped on. The spider *yokai* that attacked them at Sora's place had only spoken once. What had it meant by "heads must be taken"?

"Maybe," Mortlake suggested, "it had to take your heads back to someone to prove it had killed you?"

"Logical," Tara said. "Wasn't there a movie about that?"

"*Bring Me the Head of Alfredo Garcia*," Mortlake confirmed. "A neo-Western directed by Sam Peckinpah, I think. Taking heads was also a common samurai practice, so it fits in with the culture. That's the most likely explanation."

Craig acknowledged that it was a reasonable explanation, but it still didn't quite fit.

"Thing is," he said, "Yelbeghen has—or had—seven heads, right? And the idol was smashed, the heads were knocked off somehow, and that limited its power. I can't help but think there's a link."

There was silence while the three mulled this over before Mortlake offered some more information.

"Look, this is all very dubious, but one theory put forward by the Trustees is that Stark wants to reunite the various fragments of Yelbeghen. Now, that would imply finding the carved stone heads from the original idol. But that's not what he's been doing, is it? He's got an amulet of unknown origin and tremendous power. And he has the McIvor sword, possessed by a fierce warrior's ghost."

"And other items, presumably?" Tara put in.

Mortlake, still leaning over their seatback, gave an awkward shrug.

"That's another problem. We know Stark has collected various items over the years, but none seem to fit the bill. I have a theory that the first two missions might have been a test to see if you two were up for the job. The first was a challenge on your doorstep, just upstate, while the second involved traveling to unfamiliar territory."

Craig didn't want to credit that idea at first, but he realized it fitted with Stark's twisted, devious personality. And Stark got two very valuable items as well as tested his field operatives.

"There's so much we still don't know," he moaned. "And I still think the heads thing might be significant. A clue, if you like."

Mortlake asked them to describe the spider thing in as much detail as they could. As they did, the Englishman input data into his phone. Eventually, he made a "hmm" sound that could have meant anything.

"Trouble is," Mortlake explained, "there are quite a few spider *yokai*. Some are more dangerous than others. The one you encountered was probably a *tsuchigumo*. They can appear as human by casting some sort of glamor. That would explain how one could operate in the heart of Tokyo."

Craig had not given any thought to how a giant spider would have gotten to the maid café building. But then, he had not had much time to think about anything. It was impressive, though, that Mortlake focused on such details. His confidence in Tara's mentor had grown steadily. And, having seen them together for a while, all traces of jealousy had gone. The guy was like an eccentric uncle.

"It is the kind of monster you'd expect the cult to deploy against its enemies." Mortlake set down his phone. "It might even have been their best fighter. And you two killed it—well, you two set it on fire then Shane killed it. Well done!"

Craig felt a swell of pride, but Tara looked dubious.

"Yeah, but are there any more of those things?"

"Oh yes," Mortlake said breezily. "It's not one of a kind. There might be dozens, but we can't assume the cultists control them all."

They talked on in desultory fashion for a few more minutes while finishing their scratch meal. The train ran into a sudden, intense rainstorm that almost blotted out the view for half an hour. When the downpour eased, they were close to Aomori. Like all Japanese cities, Aomori mostly consisted of modern buildings with relatively few historic structures. Frequent earthquakes made life extra difficult for conservationists in Japan, Craig reflected, and buildings constructed to earthquake codes tended to be kind of boxy and boring. Still, better a dull but sound home or office than a stylish-looking place that might collapse on top of you.

The air was distinctly cooler when they got off the train. Aomori lay on the north coast of Honshu, and there was a slight breeze as they walked to their hotel. It was still hot, but not too bad for Craig's taste. He mentioned this to the others.

"In winter, the snow around here is about ten feet deep," Tara said. "Deeper, if you go inland. It's a weird climate."

After checking in, they set out for a café to rendezvous with one of Mortlake's contacts, a chubby young man called Nagase. They found him seated at a corner table behind an array of empty coffee cups and a plate bearing a half-eaten cheesecake. He didn't look like a Shadow Trust agent, dressed in baggy athleisure gear with scuffed sneakers. But perhaps that was the point.

Nagase was all smiles and very talkative at first, but it soon became apparent that he didn't want to guide them to the village of the dead. He spoke in slangy Japanglish laced with the odd swear word and came across as a hustler. Craig felt that the Shadow Trust had scraped the bottom of the barrel with this guy.

"There's nothing there, man," Nagase told Mortlake. "Yomimura is just fricking ruins! Old houses, overgrown streets, and fields with only weeds growing. No way the people you're looking for are still there. The cult moves around, man. The cops are pretty dumb, but other agencies are looking for those guys."

Mortlake was persistent, though. Yuta Tanaka was killed while seeking Yomimura. What's more, the snow vampire had more than hinted at impending disaster. Add to that the vision of Yelbeghen in the aurora, and there was a trail that needed to be followed.

"No, man," Nagase said. "I thought you just needed a guide for the city, the coast, temples... all the cool stuff. You want paranormal, I can show you a dozen haunted houses. There's one mansion just a couple of kilometers from here where a guy offed his family and then himself. He even did the cat, man! Place is totally cursed like in that movie with the creepy kid."

"Maybe we could just use GPS to find the village." Tara smiled sweetly at Nagase. "If this gentleman isn't keen."

"No," Mortlake said firmly. "If we're going on country roads—possibly just dirt tracks—I want a local guide. And though it's hard to believe, this chap knows the area well. He comes highly recommended."

"Yeah, I'm the best!" Nagase said with a broad grin. "But I'm not a total moron. Yomimura is bad juju. Nobody goes there."

Negotiations continued for about ten minutes, with Mortlake offering increasing amounts of cash while Nagase suggested alternatives. Craig was close to losing his temper, but Mortlake remained levelheaded. Instead of arguing further, he took out his wallet and counted out five ten-thousand-yen notes.

"That's a downpayment," he said. "You get the second half when we return."

Nagase shook his head. Mortlake counted out another five notes.

"Same when we get back," Mortlake promised.

Nagase stared at the small heap of cash. Then, he scooped it up and shoved it into his jacket pocket. Craig almost laughed at how much the guy seemed like a petty criminal from a TV show. But then, he reflected, there was a reason why some kinds of people become stereotypes.

It was only later as they climbed into a rental car that Craig worked out how much money Mortlake had given as a downpayment. One hundred thousand yen was around seven hundred dollars. He wondered if this meant Nagase was desperate for cash or had simply been faking reluctance. Given what had happened so far, Craig felt the former explanation was more likely.

He and Tara were in the backseat of the Honda SUV, with Mortlake driving and the guide riding shotgun. Nagase, after a period of sullen near silence, had recovered some of his earlier perkiness. He commented on the villages and farmsteads they passed, pointing out apple orchards and saké breweries. But he became quieter when they turned off the main highway onto a winding mountain road, only responding to questions from Mortlake.

"You guys," he muttered at one point. "You guys don't know what it's like."

"That's why we're going," Mortlake retorted. "Just keep us on the straight and narrow. You've got another hundred thousand yen to earn."

Nagase muttered something about buying a great funeral.

CHAPTER 32

VILLAGE OF THE DEAD

Three hours after setting out, they came to the end of the road when the ill-made dirt track petered out into tall, rank weeds interlaced with spiderwebs. Mortlake surprised Craig by climbing onto the hood of the SUV and surveying the valley ahead with binoculars. Then, he beckoned Nagase to join him, which the guide did reluctantly.

"Is that the village?" Mortlake asked.

Nagase took the binoculars and looked through them for a few moments, then handed them back.

"Yeah," he said. "Yeah, it's down there. That's the place."

Nagase jumped down, almost falling as he did so.

"It's odd." Mortlake climbed down more gracefully. "The place looks inhabited—or at least, there seem to be people standing around. Okay, let's get our gear."

Craig opened the back of the SUV, and they took out weapons and other gear. Craig reluctantly passed on the shuriken, having had no chance to practice, and went for daggers and an air pistol, plus a small taser.

"You'll need this, too." Mortlake handed each of them a small cylinder with a red and yellow label. It was bear repellent.

"Does this work?" Craig asked, thinking aloud.

"Let's hope we don't have to find out," Tara said cheerfully.

Craig took the bronze mirror from his backpack and looked at the racing gray clouds. A patch of sunlight played over the mountains here and there. If they waited long enough, a sunbeam might strike their particular patch of dirt, but that could take the rest of the day. He put the mirror away.

"Ready to go, I guess."

The remnants of a long-disused road to the village were just detectable underfoot as they made their way through the undergrowth. There was a slight autumn chill in the air in these northern mountains. Mortlake took the lead with Nagase close behind, followed by the two Americans. The abundant wild bushes and weeds soon blocked out the view on all sides. Craig couldn't help thinking it was ideal country from a bear's viewpoint. He quietly voiced this concern to Tara.

"Nah." She brandished the spray. "We'd hear a big animal coming well in advance. They're smart, but they can't help making noise thrashing through the undergrowth."

Craig felt reassured but kept clutching the spray.

"Is this the only road, Nagase?" he called ahead. "I mean, was it the only road?"

"So far as I know, pal," the guide replied. "But I guess there are mountain tracks as well."

Mortlake chimed in.

"If the cult set up shop here, they probably had vehicles. But it wouldn't be hard to conceal them in this."

He gestured at the chaotic greenery surrounding them.

"Maybe they hiked in," Tara suggested. "Or they might have used pack horses, right?"

"Like cowboys." Nagase grunted and slapped at a mosquito.

They broke out of the dense bush to find themselves on a broad ledge looking down on a winding stream that led downhill into the village. Yomimura consisted of around three dozen houses, all in disrepair. A couple of buildings had collapsed, their roofs caved in and weeds growing inside. But it wasn't the houses that drew Craig's eye.

It was the people.

Scattered among the houses and in the long-neglected fields were motionless figures. Some were lying down, but most stood upright. A few stood in doorways, and a couple sat together on a low wall. One leaned up against a wall alongside a bicycle.

"Ghosts?" Tara asked.

"I don't think so," Mortlake said. "I can see them too clearly. They look pretty substantial."

He handed the binoculars to Craig. The late afternoon haze made it difficult to make out details, but something was unnerving about the faces of the still figures. The route took them down into a small valley, and the village was out of sight for a couple of minutes. Then they emerged from the undergrowth on the outskirts of the settlement, and Craig saw a villager up close.

He almost laughed with relief. The figure was dressed in old, faded clothes that bulged in anatomically inaccurate ways. But that was to be expected with a scarecrow.

"Oh, my God!" Tara exclaimed. "That is creepy as hell. Why would the cult do that?"

"Maybe they didn't," Nagase said. "A lot of these places, when the population crashes and young people move away, some old lady starts filling in the gaps with scarecrows. Kind of a custom."

Mortlake took out an air pistol and pumped the lever to charge it. Craig and Tara followed suit, exchanging puzzled glances. Nagase looked even less happy.

"They *are* just scarecrows, right?" he asked.

"Maybe," Mortlake said, "but let's check. The Sanagi cult might have moved on and left some surprises."

"A supernatural booby trap?" Tara said. "Okay, not a happy thought."

Mortlake leveled his pistol at the head of a scarecrow that was about ten yards away, half-hidden in a weed-choked field. The figure wore a straw sun hat and was dressed in what Craig assumed were Japanese farm worker clothes. Mortlake fired, and an iron pellet ruffled a few strands of black string that passed for hair. A second shot jerked the hat off the scarecrow's head, and it fell backward into the weeds.

Craig raised his pistol and aimed at another scarecrow, this one standing by the roadside ahead of them. His first shot either missed or did no damage. The second caused the ragged figure to slump sideways. Tara was raising her pistol when Mortlake gently put his hand on her arm.

"Let's not waste any more ammo," he said. "I think they are what they seem. We should check in with Shane."

They stood on the outskirts of the village while Mortlake tried to contact Shane on the satellite phone. The signal was poor, even though the mountains should not have made a difference. Eventually, however, Shane responded tersely. He said that he had a lead on the cult and that they were in the north.

"We're in Yomimura now," Mortlake responded.

The speaker crackled. Shane's voice was just audible.

"No... not... Sanagi... island... mine..."

Then the phone went dead. Mortlake spent half a minute trying to recover the signal before switching off the useless device and clipping it to his belt.

"Okay, let's search the place," he said. "Weapons in each hand, I think, and ready with your PK ability."

Craig was already equipped with a pistol and a dagger. They moved forward, the three foreigners walking abreast with Nagase close behind. The guide refused to take anything other than bear spray, insisting, "I'm a lover, not a fighter."

Craig took a good look at the scarecrow he'd shot at as they passed it. Up close, it was clearly made of cloth bags stuffed with straw. The bags had perhaps contained animal feed or rice. The thing's hands were old work gloves. Its clothes were threadbare, faded, and stained. Like many of the scarecrows, it wore a straw hat that shaded its face. The eyes were just holes in the fabric, but as Craig looked into them, he got the distinct impression of something looking back. He hesitated, then walked up to the grotesque figure and jabbed it in the face with his dagger. The cloth yielded, then the iron penetrated the fabric, and yellow-brown straw leaked out.

"That'll teach him not to dress badly," Tara joked.

"Better safe than sorry," Craig replied.

One of the scarecrow's arms came up and struck Craig with a massive blow on the side of the head. The black plastic glove was not filled with straw; it felt as solid as a brick. Stunned, Craig lashed out with the dagger. More by luck than skill, the point slashed the scarecrow's face. Straw cascaded out of the collapsing head, and the thing's hat fell off, but it kept moving, swinging viciously and landing another blow that set Craig's ears ringing. He fell to his knees and then got up clumsily, focusing now on getting away from his nightmarish assailant.

A dagger flew by, gleaming in the afternoon sun, and buried itself in the scarecrow's chest. The blade wriggled as Tara used her power to gouge and shred the thing's body. The dagger vanished, then re-emerged, whirling end over end, before plunging into the scarecrow again. The figure kept coming despite the damage, its arms outstretched, seemingly determined to catch Craig in a bear hug.

Mortlake took Craig by the arm and helped him retreat while repeatedly firing his pistol into the thing's chest. There was a metallic ping as one pellet ricocheted off Tara's dagger. The scarecrow was coming apart now, one arm falling clean off while the other flailed impotently at its foes. The flying dagger appeared again, this time from behind, and curved around in a vicious arc. It took off one of the scarecrow's legs, and it toppled onto the roadway.

Tara held up her hand and caught her dagger expertly.

"Are you all right?" Mortlake asked Craig.

"Little woozy," he admitted.

"Well, focus," Tara shouted. "We've got problems."

All around them, other scarecrows were stirring.

CHAPTER 33
THE ATTACK

"We need to go somewhere defensible."

Mortlake pointed to a nearby building that was slightly larger than the others. Still supporting Craig, he started to run toward it. Tara had two daggers in the air now and used them to dismember a child-sized scarecrow in a school uniform. The attackers were moving at a walking pace, but they had already cut off the group's retreat. The car was out of reach.

The building had been a village hall or community center, judging by a notice board near the entrance and stacks of old-fashioned plastic chairs. A small atrium opened into a large meeting space, now festooned with spiderwebs and thick with dust. At the far end of the room, a fire door stood ajar.

Craig suggested using the chairs to barricade the entrance, and they quickly started piling them up. The problem was that the building had large windows opening onto the street. These were already broken in places, and soon, scarecrows were smashing what remained of the glass.

"Can they climb in?" Nagase retreated to the opposite side of the room. "Oh God, they can!"

Craig had recovered enough to help Tara, and between them, they destroyed two scarecrows. However, it took time to shred their attackers, and every second was precious. Then, an obvious solution occurred to him.

"Let's light them up! Red shirt first!"

"Okay," Tara said grimly. "Focus on the head."

The scarecrow in a red shirt was halfway through the window but had impaled itself on a shard of glass and was floundering. Craig closed his eyes and tried to calm his jangled thoughts. He imagined the molecules of the scarecrow's straw-stuffed head speeding up. He felt energy drain from him as he heated the target region. Moments later, a burning smell filled the air, and the scarecrow's lopsided bag of a head blackened and caught fire. It flopped onto the floor, the flames spreading quickly. The village had not seen rain for a while, and everything flammable was tinder dry.

"Too slow!" Mortlake shouted, still shooting with the air pistol to little effect. "There are too many."

Craig saw he was right. At least four or five assailants were climbing in through the window, and several more were shoving at the barricaded door. More scarecrows were shambling up to the building. They needed some way to stop them in one fell swoop.

"Tara," he hissed, "what about a red-hot dagger?"

It was a tough proposition. Tara looked at him for a moment in puzzlement before realization dawned.

"You move it, I'll heat it."

Craig tossed his iron dagger into the air and sent it circling the room above head height. It took Tara time to focus and heat the metal. The three retreated to the far side of the room where Nagase cowered under a boarded-up window, his eyes wide with fear, and the knuckles of one hand pressed to his mouth. About ten seconds passed as the dagger flew, and three scarecrows managed to get inside. One was so badly damaged that it crawled on all fours, but the other two closed in at an alarming speed.

"Now?" Craig said.

He'd expected the flying blade to glow red, but it seemed unaltered. Tara, her eyes shut tightly, said nothing.

"Now?" he repeated, voice almost cracking with panic.

"Do it," she said.

The dagger arced down, and Craig slowed it and put it into a spin before it impacted the closest scarecrow. He imitated Tara's trick of having it whirl around inside the thing's baggy torso. Again, the effect was delayed, but then smoke billowed from the gaping mouth and eyes of the scarecrow. It pitched forward, its arms raised in mock supplication, then collapsed in flames. Craig had already sent the hot blade through the knees of the second intruder, setting it on fire and disabling it.

The third scarecrow had cornered Nagase. Like Craig, Nagase had no mystical writings on his skin for defense. The scarecrow climbed up the man's body while Mortlake stabbed it. The thing's head was soon a ragged mess, but the body kept moving, its black rubber gloves clutching at Nagase's throat. Craig hesitated to use the flying dagger in such close quarters, but a moment later, the issue was resolved as Mortlake tore off one of the scarecrow's arms and used it to beat the grotesque entity to the floor. Moments later, what had been a deadly opponent was a heap of straw and old garments.

Craig saw a flicker of movement. A ghost, he was certain, but an odd one. It seemed to be naked, and its skin was unnaturally pale, the flesh a weird, silvery sheen. He saw two dark eyes looking at him out of a face that was like a rudimentary sketch of a person. Then, the spirit was gone.

A leper colony, he thought. *The village was a leper colony. Somehow, the cult raised the ghosts or bound them in some way.*

"Ghosts," he shouted at the others. "There are ghosts in the scarecrows. That means they can only see two of us."

Mortlake nodded curtly.

"All right; we use that. You and Nagase lure them that way, and we'll pick them off. Shut yourselves inside."

Mortlake gestured to a doorway at the far end of the room. Craig grabbed Nagase and hurried him to the fire door. The room beyond had been an office, complete with furniture, shelves, and filing cabinets. There was a small window and a second fire door that probably led outside. Craig looked back and saw that two more scarecrows had made it through the window and were hobbling toward him. They didn't get far, with Tara and

Mortlake slashing the interlopers to pieces. The scarecrows flailed desperately but had no chance. Again, just for an instant, Craig saw a pale visage as one figure collapsed in a dusty heap.

Craig stepped back from the door.

"Why do they hide?" he asked aloud.

To his surprise, Nagase answered from behind him.

"Because they hid in life. Lepers were shunned, taunted, and reviled. It's instinctive, even after death, for them to conceal their ravaged faces and bodies. Removing their coverings makes them kind of die of shame. Ironic, given that they've been dead for, well, a hell of a long time."

Craig looked around to see Nagase opening the outer door. Sunlight streamed in before the doorway was blocked by an incongruous sight. A short Japanese woman was carrying a pump action shotgun. What made the scene even more improbable was that the woman looked pregnant, with a great bulge tenting out her light summer dress. Her expression blank, the short woman leveled the shotgun at Craig and stepped to one side to admit two more people, both men, both armed.

Craig was about to turn when Nagase stepped forward and tapped him lightly on the shoulder. A wave of nausea overcame him, and he grabbed for the dust-covered desk. He tried to lash out at Nagase with psychokinesis but to no effect. It was like grasping a cloud.

"Careful, my man," Nagase said. "We need you intact for the big event."

Craig heard Tara curse from outside the room.

"Why'd they just stop?" she asked.

"I don't know," Mortlake replied.

Guns leveled, the armed men walked past Craig, followed by Nagase. More swearing from Tara.

"Don't try any of the fancy stuff." Nagase stood in the doorway. "My guys here know what to expect, and they will fire. Besides, a young lady has Craig covered. She will blow his head clean off his shoulders if you give me any trouble."

Craig stood upright, keenly aware of the shotgun barrel aimed at his face.

"Nagase, you treacherous bastard," he croaked.

The chubby young man laughed. Nagase came back into the office and looked up at Craig, shaking his head in fake bemusement.

"Oh, come on, man. I gave you a massive clue with the name," Nagase grinned. "It's not quite an anagram. We don't do those in Japanese for obvious reasons. But think about it. It should have set a few bells jingling, right? Similarity of sounds?"

Craig felt another surge of dizziness and sickness as the false guide came closer and put a hand on his arm. The man he'd known as Nagase whispered confidingly.

"You see, I am Sanagi."

CHAPTER 34

THE LAIR

Kaiju.

Buildings crashed into rubble or exploded into flames. Jet fighters swooped, firing rockets, and guns blazing, only to be shot out of the sky with crackling death beams. Men in suits and uniforms talked a lot while pretty ladies screamed and clutched frightened children. It was all so much fun, even if the corner of the screen had a kind of blurry mark on it.

Craig was staying with his grandpa and grandma for the weekend. He was on the floor of the living room, in front of the sofa where his grandpa sat nursing a root beer. The big, old TV set in the corner was showing a monster movie. King Ghidorah, a super-dragon with three heads, rampaged Japan, screeching and spitting out fiery destruction. Craig stared, enthralled, as the huge creature destroyed power lines, ripped up railroad tracks, knocked down bridges, and stomped on pathetic little tanks. Bombs and shells and bullets could not stop the mighty beast.

Grandpa had spent time in Okinawa during his Vietnam service. He explained some things to little Craig. *Kaiju* were the giant monsters in movies like this. Only Japan made such movies, Grandpa explained. The *kaiju* were popular—kids loved them. Craig could see why, even though he couldn't put his thoughts and feelings into words. Every time King Ghidorah demolished a building or wrecked a power plant, he felt a thrill of pleasure. Smashing stuff up was fun, and adults couldn't tell off the *kaiju*. King Ghidorah was like a big kid.

Having fun.

Living for the moment.

"It's just some guy in a rubber suit. You know that, right?"

Had his grandfather really said that? Was Craig mashing up memories from different times? Maybe the gentle, soft-spoken old man had been worried that his grandson would have nightmares. As the dream receded, the words stayed with Craig. Just some guy in a rubber suit. He'd found that out eventually, and it hadn't really mattered. The magic remained, that feeling of liberation through destruction. King Ghidorah, Godzilla, Mothra—each one an overgrown toddler having a tantrum.

Discomfort banished the monsters. His arms and legs were numb, and something was sticking into his left butt cheek. He shifted in his chair as he opened his eyes. His eyelids were sticky, and his vision was blurred. He felt out of it, not fully conscious. A head full of cotton wool.

He did not recognize the room he was in.

If this was a hotel, it was a weird one. He was in a roughly circular space about thirty feet across. Chairs and tables of a utilitarian design were arranged around the walls. The walls were rough-hewn rock that might have been granite. The ceiling was stone, too. And the lighting came from electric lamps strung just above head height around the chamber. At around two o'clock from Craig's position, a squarish tunnel led away into darkness.

Some sort of theme park attraction?

Then, his memory came rushing back—the village, the scarecrows, the fight, the man who called himself Sanagi.

"Oh, God," he groaned.

"You okay?"

Tara was sitting to his left. Beyond her, Mortlake was slumped forward, unconscious. They were fastened to chairs with ropes that were expertly tied. Their wrists and ankles were secured with more ropes, again elaborately knotted. Hence Craig's numbness.

"I guess." Craig shifted on the hard chair again. "Kinda groggy though."

"They drugged us, but you were already kind of out of it."

Craig recalled the way the chubby man's touch had weakened him. He tried to explain to Tara.

"Yeah," she said. "I felt some of that, but the skin characters must have reduced the effect. Well, they did until they washed the writings off us. I can just about remember that."

Craig's spirits fell a little lower. It made sense. Regardless of who Nagase or Sanagi was, he knew a lot about them. Hell, they had volunteered information, including telling him about the mystical characters on their skin. And now, they were the cult's prisoners in what looked like a very old-school dungeon.

"How long have I been out?" he asked.

"Hard to tell without my phone or watch," she replied, "but I'm guessing hours. I can only remember bits and pieces. They put us in a truck and drove us to a town. I think there might have been a boat. I remember what could have been a ship's siren."

Craig looked around the chamber again.

"Well, we're not on a boat now. Maybe down a mine?"

Tara shrugged. Craig thought back to the fight in the village hall.

"Could Nagase really be Sanagi? I mean, the actual guy, still alive by some supernatural gimmick?"

"God knows," Tara sighed. "Could be the guy's great-great whatever grandson. Or maybe it's a title now. The leader is always Sanagi."

"Like every Roman emperor was Caesar Augustus."

Mortlake had spoken. The Englishman sat upright and stared around him, groaning slightly.

"I'm sorry. I underestimated the opposition."

"Guess we all did," Craig said ruefully. "Any idea what happens next?"

Mortlake didn't answer, instead scrutinizing the room. Then, he inclined his head to one of the tables that stood along the wall to their left.

"See the mirror? I don't suppose Sanagi brought it as a souvenir."

Craig had missed it the first time he'd looked around, but he saw it now. The bronze *makyo* was propped up on the table next to a heap of books and an assortment of jars, bottles, and packets. The latter looked medicinal and presumably included the drugs they'd been given.

"Looks like they intend to keep us alive for a while." Craig tried to sound optimistic.

"Why, though?" Mortlake mused. "Evidently, they wanted the mirror, and of course, they don't want to hand over the idol. If they'd killed us in the village, our bodies would be easy to conceal. They've gone to a lot of trouble…"

An idea occurred to Craig, but he didn't want to speak it aloud. Cults sometimes went in for ritual murders. Human sacrifices. The Sanagi cult was founded to violently oppose foreign influences in Japan. Making a big deal out of murdering three foreigners would fit with that ideology.

"Maybe they want to sacrifice us," Tara said bluntly.

"Yes," Mortlake responded, "that might be the plan. But why take the trouble to transport us all this way?"

Craig had an answer.

"Maybe they want information on the Shadow Trust," he suggested. "They might think we all work for that outfit, not just you. Hey, could you use your power to untie those ropes?"

"I've tried already," she said. "I'm way too weak, thanks to the drugs. Try it yourself, though."

Craig did and found it almost impossible to focus on the rope encircling his wrists. He managed to exert his psychokinetic power but found it pathetically feeble. He couldn't even twitch his bonds let alone loosen them. Whatever drugs they'd been given kept them off-balance just enough to hamper their powers.

"Well, at least Shane is still out there looking for us," Tara said finally.

"Didn't he say something about a mine?" Craig asked.

"Yes," Mortlake agreed. "An island and a mine, if I recall correctly. So

THE ISLAND OF SHADOWS

maybe a lead in Tokyo gave him this location."

Maybe, thought Craig. It was a small consolation but all they had. He was about to loosen the ropes again when a familiar figure appeared in the doorway. Sanagi had changed into a black kimono decorated with orange flames. The two guards who followed him wore Western clothes and carried modern firearms. Again, the pregnant woman toted a shotgun while a young man wielded a pistol. Something about the two seemed off to Craig. Their faces were oddly similar, almost masklike in their lack of expression. But then, who expected fanatics to look normal?

"Well, this is nice." Sanagi leaned against the table bearing the *makyo*. "All awake and ready to hear the villain's master plan. Just like in the movies, right?"

CHAPTER 35

THE EIGHTH SOUL

"I wouldn't mind an explanation," Craig said. "I mean, you want to bring some monster back to Earth from another dimension and smash up the world, is that it?"

Sanagi smiled and picked up the bronze mirror.

"This is a wonderful thing," he said. "It provided a neat little clue that you missed. Or ignored, am I right?"

Craig thought of the faces he'd glimpsed in the mirror but said nothing.

"Yeah, and then there's this," Sanagi went on.

He picked up a book from a small pile. Craig recognized it at once as Crutchley's book of prophecies.

"Crazy name, crazy guy," Sanagi remarked, flipping through the dog-eared pages. "Professor Mortlake, I'm surprised you missed one key passage. It's buried in a great swamp of wacky religious stuff, but still."

Mortlake remained silent, gazing up coolly at Sanagi. Craig shifted in his seat and felt the mystery object digging into his butt cheek again. It was trivial but distracting. What was it? Not his keys or his phone. Sanagi began talking again.

"Ah, here it is! 'Six shall become seven and seven shall become eight and eight shall become one. Three spirits of metal, three souls of flesh, a head of shadow, and a heart of stone.' A bit obscure, but it works if you think about it. Think about a pattern that everything fits into. Kind of."

"Why bother with all this?" Craig demanded. "You're not going to let us go with a pat on the back and a ticket home, so you're just gloating over helpless victims like some crappy little gangster."

Sanagi showed anger for the first time, his round face contorting into a hostile frown. But the mood passed in a moment, and he was smiling again.

"Wrong, Mr. Ellison. So very wrong. If you'd died on the way here, it would have upset my plans a lot. Unusual people are, by definition, hard to find. I had to intervene maybe a dozen times to keep hostile *yokai* from doing you in. That slit-mouth bitch and the pesky spider still got through somehow. And all that malarkey at the shrine was annoying. Shiro was always troublesome. And a *kami* putting you through an ordeal—as if Stark's mission wasn't one already. Ridiculous. But all that interference still came to nothing. Because you're here!"

Craig struggled to make sense of what Sanagi was saying. The plump young man laughed at Craig's evident befuddlement.

"It's a complicated world, Mr. Ellison. Some of our local Japanese creatures wanted to just kill you; others wanted to strengthen you so you could kill me and my family. As if you could defeat us. It's like politics, where individuals play their own games. But I knew you'd make it through. I knew you'd prove you are the ones prophesied, and not just by Crutchley. Stark always thought you had the right stuff, but I prefer to trust my judgment."

Craig's thoughts wouldn't line up sensibly, and he was sure it wasn't just because he was sedated.

"You're working with Stark? Why? What the hell?"

"A picture is worth a thousand words, my friend."

Sanagi lifted the mirror and held it close to one of the lights strung along the walls.

"Look," he said. "See Yelbeghen, the glorious and terrible one who will free the world from this cancer you call civilization."

The reflected image was distorted by the rock wall, but it was still discernible as the seven-headed dragon. The long necks of the creature were waving, and each head was looking around. Some were snarling silently. Then, the image changed, and Craig saw his face staring back at him. Tara's face replaced it, and then Mortlake appeared. Then came three faces he did not recognize, and a fourth he did. Peregrine Stark.

"Synthesis," Mortlake said flatly. "Now I see. The fulfillment of prophecy by quest, ordeal, and sacrifice. It's the first instance I've come across in the modern world. Impressive, in a way."

Sanagi, pleased to be understood, set the mirror down.

"Exactly, Professor! Ages ago, Yelbeghen was defeated and dismembered, thanks to an alliance of human and non-human foes. The smashed idol symbolizes that setback, but the essence of a true deity is not fixed in a stone. That was never the objective. No, the eightfold god was scattered, its central soul banished to some dark world parallel to ours, while its seven lesser souls—the heads, if you like—were destroyed. A major drawback, you might think! But they can be replaced! Seven souls of power, each with unique abilities, destined to be merged with the great soul of Yelbeghen. I am the first of these. The strongest. The dominant head, if you will."

He held up the bronze mirror once more.

"Three other souls, as the prophecy foretold, are contained in material objects: this *makyo*, that haunted sword, and the sacred amulet. Three more souls are still clothed in flesh, all sitting, listening to me now, and thinking I'm a crazy fanatic who's going to murder you all. But that's so wrong."

Sanagi put down the mirror and walked over to the prisoners.

"Thanks to me, you are all going to live forever. Take it from one who has lived many lives."

Tara, who'd been looking on silently, groaned.

"So, you think you're the original Sanagi come again? The mad monk reincarnated?"

Sanagi walked over to stand beside the pregnant woman with the shotgun. He reached down and laid a plump hand on her bulging abdomen. She didn't react, didn't even blink. Her gun remained leveled on the captives.

"Yes, as a matter of fact, Ms. Pride, I am the one and only. The original. I found a way to incarnate my soul in successive generations—to become my own parent, as it were. At least two of the young ladies in my family are always ready to become vessels, just in case. And if the offspring are not required, they can still be raised as loyal acolytes."

Craig felt another wave of nausea as Sanagi's meaning penetrated his drugged brain. The man was insane, truly sick in the head. Even if what he said was true, the guy was deranged and depraved to have done it. Well, that was no surprise. How many cults are led by rational, well-balanced individuals?

"Enough talk." Sanagi lifted his hand from the woman's belly. "We have a ritual to perform, and then we will become one. Won't that be fun, eh, guys?"

Sanagi clapped his hands, and three more acolytes entered the room. They were two men and a woman, all heavily built and stony-faced. Under the watchful gaze of their leader and the armed guards, each untied a prisoner from their chair, hauled them upright, and shoved them toward the exit. Craig tried to focus his psychokinetic power on the man who held him, to no avail.

The corridor ran straight for about thirty yards and then took a sharp right. The air, already cool, became distinctly chilly. Then they were in a much larger chamber, something like a long rectangular gallery. It was around fifty feet by twenty, with a ceiling maybe ten feet high. A large mass of rusting machinery stood at the far end of the mine gallery. Between it and the entrance was a wooden altar on which lay a shrouded form. At first, Craig thought the figure was covered in a black robe. Then, he wasn't so sure. What he had thought was a garment was moving, billowing out then shrinking, to cling to the prone form. It was like a living shadow.

"What the hell is that?" Tara said.

Mortlake offered an answer.

"Darkness visible."

"Interesting, isn't it?" Sanagi walked toward the altar. "This is what your erstwhile employer called the Other when it sought him out many years ago. Unimaginative name. A prosaic mind for all his low cunning. He fondly imagined that he had been chosen for great things. But then, all dupes do. We let him think he was king, but he was never more than a pawn."

Sanagi beckoned his acolytes, and the prisoners were shoved forward to stand alongside the leader. Now that he was just a few feet away, Craig saw the face of the man on the wooden platform. It was pale in the artificial light, and the features were thin to the point of emaciation, but when the man turned to look up at him, Craig recognized him immediately. No longer young, not even middle-aged now, but with the worn and wasted features of a very old man.

"Craig… help me…" Stark croaked. "It's taking it all back. All my days, and more… much more…"

The living shadow seemed to respond to the plea. It reared up to tower over the onlookers like a pulsating cloud of pitch darkness. Then it fell onto Stark, and Craig saw black veins coursing through the man's flesh. Stark emitted a pathetic half-gasp, half-cry of despair, and then, his eyes turned glassy. His jaw hung open, slack with death. For a fleeting instant, Craig sensed a soul leaving the man's body, flitting upward to who knew what afterlife. A few words echoed in his mind, hard to make out in Craig's befuddled state.

"Pawn sacrifice," Sanagi said. "All part of the game."

CHAPTER 36
DARKNESS VISIBLE

The living shadow surged from Stark's remains to envelop Sanagi. For a heartbeat, the young man was a three-dimensional shadow. Then, the blackness seeped into Sanagi's skin, entering his eyes and mouth. The chill in the air increased, sending a shiver down Craig's spine. Sanagi smiled, his eyes still pools of darkness. He opened his mouth, and sounds emerged. It was a song in that it had rhythm and melody, but it was like nothing Craig had ever heard. If a typhoon or an earthquake had a mind, it might sing like that, he thought. Powerful, majestic, and inhuman.

Sanagi threw back his head, and the appalling, wonderful song continued, abolishing time, and making it impossible for Craig to think of anything else. He began to see visions of a world on fire, volcanos erupting, and tsunamis engulfing cities. Ships were hurled inland to wreck themselves against skyscrapers. Dams broke to inundate towns and farms. Tiny, swarming humans were swept away, obliterated in their millions. Where floods were absent, smoke from innumerable fires blotted out the sun as ruined cities burned.

The song ended.

"Well, that was bracing," Sanagi said. "Two down, six to go, eh?"

"You can't force us to participate in this lunacy," Mortlake shouted. "We have wills, and we will resist you!"

Sanagi took a step toward him.

"I'm sure you will, but not for long. None of you can harm me by any means, natural or supernatural. Given that, what's the point of trying?"

A burly cultist gripped Mortlake from behind while Sanagi reached out. One finger touched the Englishman's forehead, and he slumped, either stunned or unconscious.

"Professor Marcus Orlando Mortlake—love the middle name, by the way. A man who, in the name of doing right, has left a very long trail of corpses. A scholar and a warrior, you rode with the Wild Hunt in another world. Now, you will get to ravage this one."

The guard lowered Mortlake onto the floor as Sanagi moved on to Craig.

"My man Craig! That support group for ghosts; what a great sitcom it would have made! But that's all in the past. The future is all about power and destruction. Mortlake brought the knowledge, experience, and courage. You bring a special power over souls that will make Yelbeghen invincible to even the most powerful spirits. He will not be defeated again."

Craig tried to twist his head aside, but it was futile. Sanagi's plump finger touched his temple, and blackness flooded into him. Again, he saw destruction, but this time, it was from the point of view of the monstrous deity. Craig knew what it meant to be ancient, powerful, and pitiless. There was a joy in Yelbeghen, which had slumbered so long and was now hungry for fresh conquests. Destroying the pathetic creations of mankind was a small challenge. Civilization would be laid waste in a matter of days; weeks at most.

Something in Craig embraced the destruction. Part of his nature wanted to topple the towers of the wealthy, destroy the bankers and the politicians, level everything, and start again. It was impossible to fix the world because humans were too deeply flawed. Their science had run far ahead of their wisdom, and they had made themselves slaves of technology. With no hope of improvement and no real progress in sight, why not smash it all to the ground and begin again?

No, he insisted. *That's not me, and that's not what I truly think. Not who I am.*

"Oh, but it is," Sanagi crooned. "It is the secret, silent prayer of millions. 'Let it end, let it all come tumbling down. Let the world burn.' And now, thanks to the great one who rises through us, the world will indeed burn where it does not drown."

The Ring of Fire, Craig thought.

"Precisely," Sanagi said. "We are on a major fault line, right here. When Yelbeghen regains his strength, he will trigger seismic events on a grand scale. And then, having sewn confusion and chaos, he will stride forth and reclaim the world."

Craig, conscious but unable to move, was lowered to the stony floor. He felt his being lose definition as it merged into a greater, stranger being. He sensed Mortlake's mind burning like a hot coal, full of fury at Sanagi but powerless to act. He felt Tara, her mind confused and frightened but reaching out to his. He tried to cling to her, sensing her desperation. He touched the spirits of the mirror, the sword, and the amulet, and appealed to them. If they could combine against Sanagi... But the spirit of the sword was keen to wreak more havoc, and the others were indifferent or aloof.

And then he felt the double soul of Sanagi. Craig saw a bewildering array of faces as he sensed Sanagi's bizarre reincarnations. And now that depraved, egomaniacal soul was merging with the vast, dark force of Yelbeghen, the inhuman entity. Soon, there would be no distinct identities, only Yelbeghen. Craig felt his sense of self eaten away by the dark, ravenous soul of the monster.

Helpless, he watched as Sanagi turned his attention to Tara.

"One more soul to complete the set: a woman who has brought death to innocents. Who has already been possessed more than once. A simple matter to merge your power with ours. You have already condemned yourself in your heart, Tara Pride. Lay down your burden and become one with us."

Sanagi raised his arm but then hesitated. For the first time, Craig saw confusion in that bland countenance, and he knew why. Sanagi's powers, while great, were not invincible. He'd already admitted as much. Craig shared the cult leader's sudden awareness of an incursion. Somebody was attacking the lair.

Shane.

But not just Shane. A horde of strange beings had rallied behind the Marine. Craig recalled what he'd read about *yokai*. Some were benevolent, preservers of the order of things, and defenders of peace and the natural world. For the second time, Yelbeghen faced an alliance of human and supernatural enemies. The fearsome combination of Shane and the *yokai* was cutting a swathe through Sanagi's followers, fanatical though they were.

"No matter," Sanagi said, recovering his composure. "Let the hero strike his pose and fight his little battle. Once Yelbeghen becomes whole again, no power on Earth can harm him."

Sanagi reached out for Tara. At the same moment, Craig sensed the power he shared with her being focused, but not on Sanagi or his followers. They were too well-protected, and Tara was too weak. But she could turn her power against herself.

"No!" Craig cried.

"I'm sorry, Craig," she said.

As Tara crushed a delicate blood vessel at the base of her brain, Craig felt her mind fade, and her soul shed its material home. She was dying, and nothing could save her. All of Sanagi's power could not repair a mortally wounded body.

"Her soul will be mine!" Sanagi yelled. "She won't escape!"

Sharing the man's thoughts, Craig knew that Tara's soul could only be captured if she did not move on. Sanagi was vulnerable, if only for a few moments. The onslaught led by Shane was not just distracting him; it was sapping energy. Sanagi was fending off the small army of *yokai*, which were getting closer. His grip on his human captives was weaker. If Craig could create another distraction…

The thing in his back pocket. What an idiot he'd been. It was obvious what it was. But his psychokinetic power was ebbing along with Tara's life energy. He had seconds to act. Shutting his eyes, he concentrated on the object and felt it move. There were distant shouts, screams, and some cursing from Sanagi. Craig tried to banish all distractions, visualizing the cylinder in his pocket moving, emerging, and rising into the air.

"What are you..."

Sanagi sensed Craig's intention and reacted, but he was too slow. Craig's mental pressure triggered the bear spray. An aerosol cloud enveloped Sanagi, who doubled over as the potent chemicals filled his nose and mouth. Tara's body slumped lifelessly in the hands of the cultist, who seemed paralyzed by indecision. Sanagi, cursing and weeping, fell onto the altar next to Stark's corpse. A gunshot rang out nearby, echoing around the stone gallery.

The first *yokai* appeared. It was like a living wall, a great square block of tissue oozing black fluid from a dozen punctures. At first, Craig thought it had limbs, albeit asymmetrically distributed. But then, he realized that the creature had partially absorbed several cultists, whose arms and legs were thrashing feebly from its massive body.

Help me, Craig.

She was standing over him, very still amid the chaos. He might have mistaken her for a living person if he hadn't known. Wild energies played around the chamber like black lightning as Yelbeghen's disparate being struggled to hold itself together. Despite being blinded and confused, Sanagi was reaching out for her. Then, a many-legged nightmare descended from the ceiling on a thick, silvery rope and tried to wrap Sanagi in sticky threads. Despite this new antagonist, Sanagi continued to rage and clutch at Tara with his mind.

Weak though he was, Craig channeled his remaining energy into moving Tara on. The portal opened readily enough because she still shared his talent. A tendril of blackness flickered from Sanagi like a lizard's tongue and tried to wrap itself around her. Tara struggled, and Craig found one last iota of strength to aid her. Above her appeared a night landscape with a crescent moon, and a resplendent cloudless sky jeweled with stars.

Distant shouts, more gunshots, and strange, yelling cries. Sanagi was now encased in a glistening cocoon of pale filaments. A cultist turned and ran, only to be seized by the slit-mouthed woman, her kiss turning his face into bloody, raw meat.

All that was unimportant. Craig saw the monstrous thread of blackness grow thin, quiver, and break. Tara rose into the darkness of a tranquil night, under the myriad stars she had known and loved.

The portal closed.

EPILOGUE

"You should get out more," Billy said. "Can't stay holed up forever."

For the first time, the ghost couldn't look Craig in the eye. It made him feel awkward. He wished they could down some beers together. Just more than a week had passed since Craig had returned from Japan, and he was starting to focus on how to get on with his life.

"Seriously," the ghost went on. "Get down to Hannigan's. Talk to people. Or just go for a walk. Can't just sit around here watching trash TV and making the place look untidy."

Billy had a point. Craig sniffed his armpit and did not like the odor. He looked around the room and saw food cartons, wrappers, and packets. There were coffee mugs. There was mold.

"You did good," Billy said bluntly. "I know it feels like crap, but there were earthquakes and even a volcano somewhere. Alaska, maybe. Serious evil shit was going down, and you helped to stop it. That's the word on the street. The ghost street, anyhow. Lot of people—living and dead—are damn grateful."

Craig got up, padded into the kitchen, and poured a glass of water. The glass was dirty. He gulped a couple of mouthfuls. Then, he went into the bathroom and checked his appearance. He had put on weight, and his complexion was pale and blotchy.

All of these were facts. What he needed was emotion. Anything that could shift him out of his stinking, chaotic apartment and into the city, to move among the living in the last days of summer.

"Why did she have to die?"

Billy appeared behind him.

"She sacrificed herself like a genuine, goddamn hero. You said she was haunted by the lives she'd taken. Could say she was haunted by those victims, right?"

Craig started to protest that Tara had had no choice, that she had been possessed, but the ghost laid a hand on his shoulder. It was a gentle touch, but the chill silenced him.

"No point in trying to reason your way out of that one—it's how she felt. Guilt. Blame. We punish ourselves if we have any kind of conscience, and some of us want redemption. Settling accounts. Saving the innocent. Even if nobody ever finds out."

Craig thought of the aftermath of the battle in the mine. The *yokai*, thanks to Shane's persuasion, had spared some of the cultists. Children and several pregnant women cowered in an underground crèche. The police were summoned to the scene, and Mortlake had used his connections to steer them through a labyrinth of bureaucracy. The sword, amulet, and mirror had all been confiscated. With luck, Shane observed, they might languish forever in some evidence vault, plundered artifacts that nobody could claim.

Tara's body was returned to her family. Craig had not been invited to the funeral.

"It might not have worked out, anyway," he said.

"That's the spirit!" Billy added an inane smile and a thumbs-up gesture.

Craig managed a wan smile and traipsed back into the living room. It was disgusting. He tidied up, took off his rancid clothes, and took a shower. Billy, unusually for him, had made himself scarce for a while. The ghost reappeared after Craig had put on fresh clothes and was getting ready to go out.

"Hannigan's?" he asked.

"Just for the sake of walking there and back. Fresh air."

Billy raised a skeptical eyebrow.

"Right. When you get back—and it'd better not be too late, son!—maybe we can have a talk. About the future and shit."

Craig paused at the doorway.

"You got plans?"

Billy folded his beefy arms across his broad chest. The faded tattoo of a seven-headed dragon came into view. Craig looked away.

"No," Billy replied, "*you* should have plans. Maybe stop wasting time in this crummy town and take your show on the road."

Craig had no idea what he meant and said so.

"God, it's simple enough," Billy sighed. "There are people who need help all over this fair land of ours. The living *and* the dead. From sea to shining sea, right? So, set yourself up as a freelancer—call yourself a psychic consultant or some BS—and go help them. Get paid for it. Have adventures. Hell, maybe meet someone and fall in love. Yeah, I know. Way too soon. But one day it won't be too soon. Maybe that day shouldn't dawn here. Too many memories. Catch my drift?"

Craig smiled a little wearily.

"Yeah, your drift is caught. I'll think about it. Over a couple of beers."

Check out these best-selling series from our talented authors:

GHOST STORIES

RON RIPLEY
BERKLEY STREET SERIES
MOVING IN SERIES
HAUNTED COLLECTION SERIES
DEATH HUNTER SERIES

IAN FORTEY
JIGSAW OF SOULS SERIES
CULT OF THE ENDLESS NIGHT SERIES

SUPERNATURAL SUSPENSE

A. I. NASSER
SLAUGHTER SERIES
SIN SERIES

DAVID LONGHORN
NIGHTMARE SERIES
ASYLUM SERIES

SARA CLANCY
THE BELL WITCH SERIES
BANSHEE SERIES

For a complete list of our new releases and best-selling horror books, visit ScareStreet.com or scan the QR code below!